the
sanibel
sunset
detective

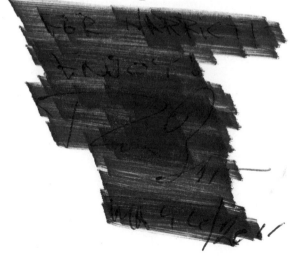

Also by Ron Base

Fiction

Matinee Idol
Foreign Object
Splendido
Magic Man
The Strange

Nonfiction

The Movies of the Eighties (with David Haslam)
If the Other Guy Isn't Jack Nicholson, I've Got the Part
Marquee Guide to Movies on Video
Cuba Portrait of an Island (with Donald Nausbaum)

www.ronbase.com

Contact Ron at
ronbase@ronbase.com

the sanibel sunset detective

a novel

RON BASE

Library and Archives Canada Cataloguing in Publication

Base, Ron, 1948 –
The Sanibel Sunset Detective / Ron Base.

ISBN 978–0–9736955-4-0

I. Title

PS8553.A784S36 2010   C813'.54   C2010-907341-X

West-End Books
80 Front St. East, Suite 605
Toronto, Ontario
Canada M5E 1T4

Cover Design: Bridgit Stone-Budd
Text Design: Ric Base
Electronic formatting: Ric Base

For Ric

Private investigators and private investigative agencies serve in positions of trust. Untrained and unlicensed persons or businesses, or persons not of good moral character, are a threat to the public safety and welfare.

-Florida Department of Agriculture and Consumer Services

"So you're a private detective," she said. "I didn't know they really existed, except in books. Or else they were greasy little men snooping around hotels."

–Raymond Chandler, The Big Sleep

The world breaks everyone and afterward many are stronger at the broken places.

-Ernest Hemingway

1

The advertisement appeared simultaneously in the Want Ads sections of the *Sanibel Island Reporter* and the *Fort Myers News-Press*.

Sanibel Sunset Detective
Professional Investigation
Discretion Guaranteed
1159 Causeway Rd.
Sanibel Island, Fl.
Phone 239-472-2348

A week later, Rex Baxter, president of the Sanibel-Captiva Chamber of Commerce, in what was becoming something of a morning ritual, shambled into Tree Callister's office and presented him with a Starbucks Grande Caffe Latte.

"I'm sick and tired of waiting on you," Rex said.

"What's scary is, I'm starting to look forward to this," Tree said.

"It's not like I feel sorry for you or anything," Rex said. He eased himself into the only empty chair in the tiny office. "You coming to the end of a wasted life with nothing to show for it."

"You've got a point there," Tree said.

Rex was tall with wavy grey hair that made him look like a local TV anchorman, which, in fact, he had been for many years at WBBM-TV in Chicago. Well, not an anchor, exactly. Rex was the weatherman for the station's late afternoon newscast. Before that, he had been a movie actor in 1950s B-pictures. He came to Chicago to host an afternoon movie show. That's how Tree and Rex knew each other. Tree had interviewed him for his newspaper, the *Sun-Times*. They had been friends ever since.

Originally from Oklahoma, and proud of it, Rex now was almost as much a part of Sanibel as the palm trees and the beaches. Tree, on the other hand, was not part of anything. Tree was an ex-newspaperman who didn't know what to do with himself. Rex let Tree have the office upstairs at the Chamber of Commerce Visitors Center so he could get started in the detective business. Rex thought Tree was out of his mind, but the office was empty, and it would mean there was another body around to answer the phone when everyone was at lunch.

Rex said, "Okay, try this one on for size. Your favorite private detective movie."

Tree thought about it a moment before he said, "*Twilight.*"

Rex scratched at one of the wattles that had developed beneath his chin. "*Twilight*? That vampire movie?"

"This is another *Twilight*. The better *Twilight*."

"Never even heard of it."

"Paul Newman is an ex-cop, ex-drunk in Los Angeles, living with famous husband-and-wife movie stars played by Gene Hackman and Susan Sarandon. Hackman is Newman's best friend. The scenes between the two of them are priceless. Sort of like us, Rex."

"You're Newman, I'm Hackman, is that it?"

"It's Newman's last starring role. He's too old for it, but he's Paul Newman one final time, a little tired, a little world weary, but not giving into it, beating on, trying to make the best of what he's been handed."

"Like you, Tree."

"Except I'm not Paul Newman. The tragedy of my life. What guy of a certain age doesn't look at Paul Newman on the screen and identify with him? Everyone wants to be Cool Hand Luke."

"What's *Twilight* about?"

"It's about coming to the end, but if you mean the plot, who knows? If you can remember the plot of a private detective movie, then it's probably not a very good private detective movie."

"Come on," Rex said. "Private detective movies are nothing but plot."

"Oh, yeah? What's *The Big Sleep* about?"

Rex was silent. "Well, it's about Humphrey Bogart and Lauren Bacall."

Tree grinned. "And that's more than enough plot for any movie. I rest my case."

They were interrupted by the thump of footsteps on the stairs leading to Tree's office. They both turned to see a boy in a Tampa Bay Rays baseball cap appear in the doorway.

"This the Sanibel Sunset Detective Agency?"

"It is indeed," Tree said.

"I want to talk to a detective," the boy said.

Rex winked at Tree and stood. "I've got to get over to the Ding Darling Education Center so I can finish making my gun."

"Your gun?" Tree said.

"A rifle, actually. A replica of the real thing. But it works. Talk to you later."

Rex ambled out past the boy who remained in the doorway. Tree waved at him. "Come on in and have a seat."

The boy ventured tentatively into the room. He was African American. A backpack hung from his shoulders. He wore the usual island uniform: khaki shorts and a T-shirt that was too big for him, with a picture of a fish and "Sanibel Island" printed across the front.

"You are the detective guy?" As though he couldn't quite believe it.

"I wouldn't lie to you," Tree said.

"You don't look like a detective."

"How are detectives supposed to look?"

"Younger," the boy said.

He perched on the edge of the chair vacated by Rex, his head barely visible over the desk.

"So like I could hire you, right?"

"What's your name?"

He hesitated before he said, "Marcello."

"Marcello?"

"Like the Italian actor."

"Marcello Mastroianni?"

The boy shrugged. "My mom said the Italian actor."

"Okay, Marcello. Aren't you a little young to be hiring detectives?"

"How old do you have to be?"

"How old are you?"

Marcello hardly paused before he said, "Twenty-one."

"You shouldn't lie to a detective," Tree said.

"How do you know I'm lying?"

"I'm a detective," he said.

"You think I'm young because you're so old."

Tree looked at him.

"It's my mom," Marcello said.

"What about her?"

"I want you to find her."

"I see. Where is your mom?"

A look of impatience crossed the boy's delicate features. "If I knew that, I wouldn't have to hire you."

"That's true," Tree had to admit.

"I got a card from her," he said.

"Okay."

"Would you like to see it?"

Tree said he would. The boy swung the backpack off his shoulders and from it fished out a small blue greeting card. He handed it to Tree. Fumbling in his shirt pocket, Tree located his glasses and balanced them on the end of his nose. Marcello made a face.

"What are those?"

"The glasses? They're glasses."

"You wear glasses?"

"For reading. Just for reading." Did he sound a tad defensive? He repositioned the glasses on the bridge of his nose and looked at the card. There was a small white heart in the bottom right-hand corner.

Tree opened it up. The handwriting in the interior was neat and feminine.

Hello, my little love,

I know you haven't heard from me for a while, and I'm sorry. I should have written earlier. I love you very much, I want you to know that. I haven't forgotten about you. I think about you all the time. I will be coming for you soon, I promise, darling. In the meantime, please be strong and brave, and remember that you are loved more than you will ever know.

Mommy

Tree handed the card back to Marcello who carefully replaced it in his backpack. Tree took his glasses off and put them back in his shirt pocket. "When did you get this?" he asked.

He looked uneasy. "Can you find my mom or not?"

"Okay, Marcello, it doesn't seem as though she's missing since she recently sent you a letter. She says she's coming to get you and you should be patient."

"So what does that mean? You won't find her?"

"If your mom really is missing, you should go to the police."

"I don't like the police."

"Nonetheless, they are the people best equipped to find your mom—if she really is missing."

"What's the use you being a detective and everything if all you do is tell people to call the police?"

"I don't tell that to everyone," Tree said. "Only twelve-year-old boys."

"Well, I'm twenty-one."

"Nonetheless, I think you should go to the police."

The kid got up from the chair. Even then he didn't rise up that much above the desk, Tree noted. A small twelve. Maybe he wasn't even twelve. The boy re-slung the backpack on his shoulders.

"You're old and I don't think I like you," he said.

"Detectives aren't supposed to be liked," said Tree.

"Then you must be a great detective."

Tree couldn't help but smile. He decided to try to be helpful. "Your mother sounds like a nice person, Marcello."

"That's why I want to be with her."

Would you like me to call the police for you?"

Marcello shook his head. "I told you already. I don't like the police."

"That's right. I forgot."

Marcello went out. Tree put his glasses back on, wondering if he should let the boy go. He heard him clomp back down the stairs. Tree swiveled around to stare out the window into the parking lot, still wondering what he should do. Marcello swept past astride a red bicycle. Then he was gone. The kid was from around here, no doubt. He'd be all right. Probably mom and dad were divorced. The boy lived with his father and maybe a stepmother. He missed his real mom, that was all, and then he got that letter, and maybe his mom should have showed up by now and hadn't.

That was it. No more to it than that.

The boy's comments about age irritated him. He wasn't that old, was he? He still had most of his hair and that was a plus, and it had remained mostly black, albeit shot through with grey streaks. He liked to think that just made him more distinguished. He had put on some weight in the last few years, but he worked out three or four times a week and being tall like Rex, six feet, two inches, he was, he believed, able to carry a few extra pounds. Or was he deluding himself? It was the age of delusion. He told himself he did not feel sixty. However sixty was supposed to feel.

In addition to telling himself he did not feel sixty, he also repeated to himself how lucky he was—lucky to have met his wife, Freddie, lucky to have experienced the last great days of Chicago newspapers. He had started out at the *Daily News* and when that folded, a victim of the world's lack of interest in an afternoon newspaper, he had gone over to the *Sun-Times* where he toiled away happily. He knew Mike Royko, the legendary Chicago columnist, well, he didn't *know* Royko, could anyone? But he would nod at Tree when they encountered each other in the city room, and Mike would say, "Hi, there, Tree." A cub of a reporter, barely out of his teens, Tree was thrilled.

Newspaper*men*—and they were mostly men—wore ties, never fully tied, and white shirts with the collar button undone. They punched at Underwood typewriters with two fingers, and editors yelled "Copy!" and everyone smoked incessantly so that a pall of grey smoke hung constantly over the battlefield that was the city room.

They drank draught beer for lunch at Riccardo's, the watering hole of choice, bitching about the corruption of the Daley political machine that ran Chicago forever—Richard *J.* Daley, that is, not the son, Richard *M.* Daley, who, when he was mayor, gentrified the city to the point where Tree barely recognized it. Tree loved all of it, loved it too much, at the expense of things like family.

He loved it so much he hung around long enough to see it all change, which is to say he hung around too long.

His mind drifted to another popular topic lately, the mediocrity of his misspent life. He had a lot of time to ponder that subject. He thought about it in the dispassionate way a man who has recently turned sixty must consider these things. After all, no matter how you cut it, the bulk of a lifetime, its essential weight, already had been mounted on the scale and weighed. The weight in his case was light. The future did not promise much more heft. How could it? There was not, he had to admit, a whole lot of future left to consider. A curious thing to realize that there was more behind you than there was ahead.

He did not think like this out of any sense of depression—Tree could not honestly say he was depressed—more of resignation. This was the way it had turned out, and there was not much he could do about it.

Well, there was one thing. You could open your very own detective agency. Not a universal response to the aging process, but his response. So far it had been pretty quiet. Not unexpected since he had no experience as a detective. Someone asked him how many operatives the Sanibel Sunset Detective Agency employed. Operatives? There was only one operative. W. Tremain Callister—Tree—he was *the* Sanibel Sunset Detective.

One detective, then, and zero clients. Tree shifted his gaze away from the window.

You could hardly count the kid. Marcello? Probably home by now. Hopefully, someone was giving him a hug and pouring him a glass of milk and he was okay. Probably forgotten all about his visit to a real live private detective.

Except he wasn't much of a detective. Maybe he handled the boy the wrong way. Certainly he was capable of mishandling kids. All you had to do was ask his. Suppose Marcello wasn't home getting a hug and a glass of milk? Suppose someone was knocking him around and his lost mom and that letter were all he had to hang on to? Could his mother really be missing? A lot of kids' parents were missing in action, he supposed. Maybe he should have taken him home and made sure he was all right. He would be fine. Maybe it wasn't even serious. Maybe the kid was playing some sort of weird joke.

Who would be crazy enough to hire Tree Callister, anyway? Paul Newman, sure. He could find your mom and solve your problems because he was Paul Newman. But Tree Callister? What could he ever do for you?

2

Tree left the office late in the afternoon and got into his battered yellow Volkswagen Beetle convertible. His wife Freddie's red Mercedes was at the garage for a tune-up. Tree's job today was to pick her up and drive her home. He was a private investigator. He could handle that.

The traffic heading off the island on Causeway Boulevard was already heavy. He turned on to Periwinkle Way and came along to Dayton's, the late afternoon sun glinting off his windshield, Elvis on the radio singing "Jailhouse Rock." Lately, he had begun listening to one of the local classic rock radio stations for whom time stopped at the end of 1969. He tried to tell himself this had nothing to do with nostalgia for his fading past, but of course it did. "Jailhouse Rock" made him think of the Elvis Presley concert at Cobo Hall in Detroit in 1970, the excitement of seeing a legend who had not performed for ten years, of witnessing a comeback that people still talked about.

Well, people of a certain age still talked about.

Tree supposed his increasing reliance on pop standards also had something to do with his lack of identification with what was happening on contemporary radio. He hated that, hated that the world appeared to be drifting, that what was noise to him was the music of the day to a generation. He was beginning to feel like his parents, the people he swore he would never emulate.

Dayton's Supermarkets had been part of the Fort Myers-Naples-Tampa area since Ray Dayton took over the company after he came back from Vietnam in 1974. Ray's grandfather had started the business on Sanibel in the 1940s. Ray looked more like his granddad every day .

Mr. Ray, as he liked to be called, had served his country fighting in Vietnam. Everyone knew that. A sentence containing Mr. Ray's name invariably also carried the information that he was a brave veteran who had been to Nam. That's what everyone said. He had not been to Vietnam. He had been to Nam.

Mr. Ray was talking to Sam Mercer as Tree drove into the parking lot. Sam owned a small resort on Tarpon Bay. He was also president of the Kiwanis Club. Sam and Mr. Ray watched Tree park the Volkswagen. Conversation ceased as he got out of the car and started toward them. Sam removed his sunglasses to get a better look at the interloper. Mr. Ray's short-cropped white hair glistened in the sunlight. His face was like a slab of stone carved out of a windstorm.

"Hey, Tree."

"How are you, Ray?"

Sam said, "How's the detective business, Tree?"

"Busy, busy," Tree said with a smile.

Neither man smiled back. Ray Dayton said, "Freddie's inside, Tree."

"Thanks."

"You should drop around to Kiwanis, Tree." Sam Mercer spoke slowly, as though addressing someone with learning disabilities. "We could use a detective. Might be good for your business."

"Thanks Sam, I appreciate that."

He could feel their eyes on him as he headed toward Dayton's: *the guy's an idiot.*

Tree stepped into the supermarket's air conditioned coolness. Freddie appeared in a blur of summer linen hurrying along aisle one (pretzels, chips, beer). Tree tried to imagine her with a pretzel or a beer and couldn't do it. She was on her Blackberry.

"Yes, but Terry any way you look at it, our shrink is too high. We've got to do better. I want a meeting with him. How about tomorrow? Ten o'clock. See you then, Terry."

She got off her phone and her smile brightened. "There you are."

She kissed him quickly on the mouth, a wifely peck, acceptable in public. Tree liked the way she did it. He liked everything about Fredericka Stayner, known to everyone as Freddie—the way she walked, the sweep of her honey-colored hair, the deep green of her eyes, her elegance, the effortless intelligence. Every time he thought of her, it made him smile. After ten years of marriage, he was still smiling.

"The Mercedes isn't going to be ready until tomorrow."

"Then it looks like I'm going to have to drive you home."

"I hate driving in that car," she said. "I wish you'd let me buy a new one."

"It's my pride and joy," Tree said. "The only thing I have in this world."

"You have me," Freddie said.

"Better even than the Beetle," he said, taking her hand.

"I don't rattle, and I'm not constantly blaring old rock and roll tunes."

"I don't listen to old rock all the time," Tree maintained.

"Yes, you do. The next thing you'll try to make me watch *The Guns of Navarone* again."

"What a lovely way to spend an evening," he said.

She rolled her eyes and squeezed his hand.

Freddie was Tree's fourth wife. He could hardly believe it. Four wives? Impossible. Movie stars married four times. Rock musicians. Not Tree Callister. Years ago, a callow young Chicago reporter, he had interviewed Henry Fonda. As afternoon shadows lengthened across Fonda's still youthfully iconic face, the face of Tom Joad in autumn, the actor expressed anguish over his four marriages. He was ashamed of the divorces. Tree wondered how it was possible to deal with all the emotional and financial complications that many breakups must have entailed.

Now he knew.

He married the first time in his early twenties. What the hell had he been thinking, marrying that young? He wanted the hard-drinking Hemingwayesque newspaper reporter, not a happily married family man. His first wife, Judy, young, dutiful, naïve, desiring all the traditional trappings of marriage, including a husband who came home at night. They produced two children, Raymond and Christopher, before everything fell apart—the bad husband exiting the bad marriage, leaving behind crying children and an angry wife.

Rex Baxter had introduced him to his second wife, Kelly Fleming, a Chicago newscaster who lit up any room she entered. Tree was mesmerized. He remained mesmerized; Kelly less so. A recipe for disaster that ended after three years. Then came Patricia Laine, the entertainment editor at the *Sun-Times*. She threw him out a little over a year after they married and went off with the editor of the paper, an upgrade.

After Patricia, he was more or less single for the next five years, except for the live-in law student twenty years his junior. The less said about that, the better.

His marriages, he decided, were rites of passage, necessary journeys on the way to destiny in the form of Fredericka Stayner. Not that he believed in destiny—except where Freddie was concerned. That had to be destiny. It could be nothing else.

Friends introduced them at a Gold Coast dinner party. She was a high-powered, hard-driving, department store executive, stunning in Ralph Lauren. As soon as Tree laid eyes on her, he wanted to marry her. That, Freddie said later, was part of his problem. Tree saw a car he liked, he wanted to marry it.

They chatted over pompano and crunchy asparagus. She hadn't seen the Matisse exhibit at the Art Institute of Chicago.

Had he? No, hadn't had a chance. Was he even intending to go? he thought to himself. No, but what difference did that make? He suggested they meet the next afternoon. They could look at it together. She delivered what was to be one of many cool, green-eyed appraisals. Green is the rarest eye color, he thought inanely. Where had he read that? He held his breath. She nodded. Two o'clock? Two o'clock would be fine.

He counted the moments until he met her on the steps of the Art Institute. They wandered together through the exhibit, not saying much. Matisse must have been in a particularly slap-dash and simple mood in the period following his return from Morocco but before heading off to the South of France, all the while bemoaning the work that went into his painting. Not only was comedy hard, but according to the never-happy Matisse, so was painting.

Tree marveled at how self-contained Matisse was. His art was all, nothing else existed, not even the world war in progress down the road from his Paris studio. It never seemed to occur to Matisse that the public might not care for his images. What difference did that make? No focus groups in Matisse's world, Tree observed. Freddie laughed and said she didn't much care for this part of Matisse.

They wandered down to American Art Before 1900. Unlike the Matisse exhibit, which was so crowded people jostled for position in front of the paintings, here they were alone except for a bored-looking guard, and even he disappeared after a few minutes.

Nobody gave a hoot about American art before 1900, Tree supposed. Not even for Frederic Remington's stuff which Tree loved because Remington evoked the John Ford westerns he grew up with. Westerns? Freddie groaned. She hated westerns. Who even thought about westerns these days? Tree was willing to forgive her that particular shortcoming. He was willing to forgive her anything. They kissed in front of Remington's "End of the Trail" bronze. Tree kept an eye on the lone Indian warrior astride his horse, head bowed in defeat. Today, he was the warrior victorious, if only briefly. After that, they couldn't stop kissing. They had been kissing ever since.

Freddie had been married twice before. The starter marriage was packaged with all the traditional trimmings: the bride in white, the bridesmaids in pink; the groom and best man in baby-blue tuxedos; the band at the Palmer House reception with featured accordions playing "Welcome to My World." The new husband got too drunk on the wedding night to do anything but throw up in the bridal suite.

The second marriage, as second marriages tend to be, was more serious business. The guy was ten years older, well-to-do, with boutique hotels in Chicago, New York, and Los Angeles. They had a daughter together, Emma. Glenn—that was number two's name—was a controlling drunk who, when things didn't go his way, threatened to kill his wife. Freddie could never be sure if he was serious, but she wasn't taking any chances and got out of the marriage, taking Emma with her.

Tree had to work on Freddie, behave himself in ways he had never before behaved, court her properly, show up when he said he would. None of that was a problem. All the things he could never achieve in his other relationships, were achieved effortlessly with Freddie.

She finally agreed to marry him, commenting that the last thing she expected was to marry some guy who had been married three times before. Not that the two strikes against her were anything to be proud of.

If it was any consolation, Tree said, he never expected to be that guy.

———

Freddie waved at Mr. Ray as they headed toward the car. "I'm meeting Terry at ten tomorrow morning."

"The shrink rate is fine," he called back.

"No it's not," she said. Mr. Ray gave the dead-eyed stare usually reserved for Tree. "Honestly," she said in a low voice, "There are days when I could murder that man."

"Most days I think the Ray Man wants to kill me."

"He continues to believe that all you have to do is pull the trucks up to the back door and unload them."

"But he hired you," Tree said. "And he's been in Nam."

"In his head he knows that. In his heart, I am the irritating city broad who has never unloaded a truck."

"Or served in Vietnam," Tree said.

On the way home he told Freddie about his first client. "Wonderful," she said in the flat voice she employed when she wasn't paying attention to him. Not that he blamed her. Freddie had not discouraged his move into detecting, as she would not discourage anything her husband decided to undertake, but she didn't encourage it, either.

"Unfortunately, he was only twelve years old."

That got her attention. "You're kidding. He was twelve?"

"Actually, he may not even have been twelve."

"What did he want you to do?"

"Find his mother."

"What did you tell him?"

"I told him he should go to the police."

"You didn't take him to the police yourself?" A hint of disapproval.

"I should have, shouldn't I?"

"A little boy so desperate to find his mom he goes to a detective. Kind of sad."

The observation came without judgmental inflection. Except he knew damn well he was being judged, and not positively.

"I should have handled it better."

"Well, hopefully he's all right. What's his name?"

"Marcello."

"That's it, Marcello?"

"After the Italian actor."

"He's named after Marcello Mastroianni?"

"Apparently."

"But you didn't get his last name."

"That's all he said," Tree said, kicking himself for not getting the kid's last name. "Like I said, I didn't handle it so well."

They crossed Blind Pass onto Captiva Island. Their house

on Andy Rosse Lane like most of the newer houses in the area, was built above the garage so that in the event of a hurricane—Charley in 2004 remained fresh in everyone's mind—flood damage would be minimal. Such were the concessions you made to life in the tropics, Tree reflected. You lived in air, floating, not tethered to anything.

The house was lost in a profusion of palm trees and hedges. A sitting room with big windows showing a view of the sea dominated. A good-sized kitchen had been recently updated with de rigueur granite counters and stainless steel appliances. When they moved in, they had redone the place in bright Mediterranean tones and hung the paintings they'd collected—the oversized poster for the bad French movie Tree had written in Paris was consigned to a wall in the laundry room.

Freddie cooked turkey burgers on their Weber barbecue using real charcoal. Gas barbecues were nothing but outdoor stoves, she said. Not really barbecues at all. She had a glass of chardonnay.

After dinner they sat on the terrace overlooking the pool they never used, watching one of the spectacular sunsets tourists came from all over the world to see. Tree watched that sun in all its dying glory and decided life was not so bad.

He thought no further of twelve-year-old boys looking for their mothers.

3

A tall man with dark hair in a white linen suit waited for Tree when he arrived at the office the next morning. Tree couldn't take his eyes off the linen suit. It fell gracefully along the contours of his visitor's slim torso. Linen wrinkled so easily, thought Tree, who did not own a lot of linen—he didn't own any. How could this guy's suit not wrinkle?

The tall man smiled when he saw Tree. The smile was as effortless as the way he wore that linen suit. The smile could not hide the threatening air that hung around him like a shroud on a coffin.

"Did you know," he said in a polite voice tinged with the luck of the Irish, "that the osprey used to be known as a fish hawk."

Tree removed his glasses. "I read that somewhere."

"Fish hawk," the man in the linen suit said. "I like that better than osprey. Fish hawk sounds tougher somehow, more primal. Don't you think?"

"I'm sorry," Tree said. "I didn't get your name."

"They mate for life, you know. The fish hawks."

"I didn't know that," Tree said.

"They build nests of sticks, and then they go back to it each year, always adding sticks. Some of these nests, as you might imagine, grow quite large."

"What can I do for you?" Tree said.

The man's smile tightened. "Pretty busy, son?"

"I have a number of clients to do deal with this morning," Tree said in the formal voice he adopted when lying through his teeth.

"Here's something else that's interesting about the fish hawk or the osprey, if that's what you want to call it. Once the male and female have courted and come together, the male devotes himself to providing the female with fresh fish. Romantic don't you think? Making sure his wife is fed properly. Nice."

"I've learned a great deal about the osprey this morning," Tree said. "Fascinating. But maybe we should get down to business."

"Down to business," the man said. "Interesting choice of words. Yes, I suppose we should get right down to business. You and me we've got something in common, you know."

"A love of osprey?"

"Chicago, son. The second city."

"You're from Chicago?"

"As I understand you are. Where from exactly?"

"Around and about. Lincoln Park, mostly."

"Small world. I lived on Clark, a block away from the garage where the St. Valentine's Day Massacre took place."

"Is that so?"

"Of course, it's a parking lot now. But I learned a lot in Chicago, I did. The Windy City. Indeed. Well, that's pleasant enough. Old pals and all."

"You spend a lot of time here looking for people from Chicago?"

The tall man laughed. "I don't spend any time at all. I got out of that town a long time ago. A young lady broke my heart. But isn't it the way of the world?"

Tree just looked at him. He didn't like the way this was going. He put his glasses on again, hoping they would give him a better view of his visitor. The view did not improve.

"Okay, this is the business I want to deal with this morning," the tall man said. "I require your help."

"Something to do with fish hawks?"

"With locating a certain person."

"A person. What kind of person?"

"The kind of person who makes me very angry running away like that."

"Another heartbreaker?"

"A man can only take one of those in a lifetime."

"You want me to find this person for you?"

"In a manner of speaking, yes."

"It would help to know your name," Tree said.

"My name? I didn't tell you my name?"

"I'm afraid not."

He laughed out loud. "Isn't that damnedest thing? All this talk about Chicago, I forgot. Reno, son. Reno O'Hara."

"Tree Callister."

"Yes, I know that. Mr. Tree Callister from Chicago. Tree. A funny name for a man. I hope you don't mind me saying that."

"You wouldn't be the first person who has commented on it over the years."

Reno O'Hara glanced around the room as though looking for an item he had mislaid. "Tell me something, Tree."

"What's that, Reno?"

"When is the last time anyone hit you?"

Tree looked at him.

"I suspect it was in a schoolyard, right? Something like that. Or maybe at a bar when you were a young man. You know, pushing and shoving after too many drinks. Maybe over a girl. Youthful fights, they are almost always over a girl, don't you think?"

Tree did not respond.

"But I'm not talking about things like that, minor scuffles. I'm talking about really getting hit—a fist in the mouth, for example. Or someone who knows how to do it, punching you in the stomach. You really get hit, and you feel it. None of this stuff like in the movies where the hero shakes it off and then comes back and lands the punches that defeat his opponent.

I'm talking about getting hit like it's a freight train running into you, like you go to the hospital, and they have to rewire your jaw or tape your ribs. Recovery takes weeks accompanied by such tremendous hurt, the doctor must prescribe powerful painkillers. You are on, like workman's compensation, although maybe a guy like you, a guy named for a tree, who is a loser and doesn't earn shit, there is no workman's compensation."

Tree was frozen in place. Reno O'Hara rewarded Tree's tense silence with an understanding smile.

"So you tell me what I need to know, and we avoid all the unpleasantness I have just discussed with you. That makes sense don't it, Tree?"

Reno was right. No one had ever hit him. Not even in school. Or during a barroom brawl. What sort of newspaperman was he, anyway, that he never got into a fist fight? Reporters in his day fought all the time; they brawled in the street, for God's sake. But somehow he had avoided all that. When he got drunk during his drinking days, he transformed into the world's nicest guy. Good old Tree. Well, right now good old Tree was in trouble, and he wasn't quite certain how to handle it.

"Look, we've still got a bit of a problem here, Reno." Tree tried his best to sound reasonable. That's what would work in a situation like this. Reason.

"What problem is that?"

"I don't know what you're talking about."

Reno's face went dark. Tree found himself being lifted off his chair and slammed against the wall. His reading glasses spun away. A framed photograph of a bikini-clad beauty catching a marlin crashed to the floor. Reno's taut face deployed in a shower of bursting stars.

"You tell her. Okay? Tell her."

"Tell who?" Tree managed to gurgle.

"She comes back, no hard feelings. Everything is A-okay again. Got that?"

"A-okay. Right."

Reno let go of him and backed away. His face no longer

resembled a storm brewing. A smile played at his lips. "Where did she find you, son? What is there? Some sort of Florida Loser Club? You just call up and they send over a loser?"

"Yeah, that's it all right," Tree agreed, trying to catch his breath.

"Let me give you some advice. Get away from this shit. As far as you can. You know what I can do to a guy who gets in my way. This is what I do, son. I scare myself sometimes. So make sure you don't get on my wrong side again, okay?"

"Okay."

"Just stay away from her."

And then Reno O'Hara was gone. Tree stood there. Gulping for air.

4

Freddie and Tree had married five days before the *Sun-Times* downsized him or, as they used to say in a more simple time, before they fired him. The timing couldn't have been better for Tree, Freddie observed. Five days later, and she might have reconsidered. Freddie smiled when she said this. He was pretty sure she was joking.

Downsized.

Interesting word. *Downsized.* After twenty-five years in the newspaper business. Finished. Left feeling alone and curiously hollowed out as though, abruptly, he no longer was anyone, a man without an identity. He used to be a reporter, a journalist—a real live Chicago newspaperman. Now he was, what?

He didn't know.

He kicked around writing magazine pieces while he looked for other newspaper jobs. There weren't any. They were getting rid of guys his age, not hiring them. Everyone was being ushered out the door. Everyone was looking for a job. The end of an era. The end of the world, at least the end of the newspaper world he had known all his adult life, the world he thought—they all thought—would never end. Newspapers reported the catastrophes. They were not supposed to be the catastrophes.

He wrote scripts. The good scripts never got made. The bad scripts became low-budget thrillers, running to a similar theme: a newspaper editor was accused of a murder he didn't commit; a magazine editor was accused of a murder she didn't commit.

Soon enough the bottom fell out of the low-budget straight-to-video market that had kept him more or less employed—or perhaps producers realized he wasn't much of screenwriter. Maybe it was a combination of both things.

He had sat at home reflecting on his lack of talent, much the same way he now sat in his office, mouth dry, stomach churning, the stars finally deserting his thick head. He found his reading glasses on the floor, folded them, and put them into his pocket as he listened to the muted voices of the tourists downstairs. He revisited the encounter with Reno O'Hara, trying to locate the part where he had taken control, refused to allow himself to be pushed around.

He couldn't find that part.

Every time he inspected his actions, he felt worse. He was no better than the teenage Tree in fear of those long ago encounters with punks in leather jackets lurking in the designated No Man's Land one dreaded block from school. He felt violated. He wanted to talk to someone. But who? Freddie? He talked to her about everything, but not this, not right now, not until his pulse settled and his heart stopped racing.

He went down the back stairs and stumbled outside, half expecting to find Reno waiting for him. But no Reno. Just another tourist family climbing out of their van headed into the visitors center. Mom and dad and two adorable children, unaware of the evil lurking beneath the Florida sun. Just as well they didn't know. Tree didn't want to spoil their vacation.

He took deep breaths. He wasn't hurt. A little shaken up, that's all; his pride wounded. Well, wounded pride never killed anyone. If he still drank he would go to a bar, calm his nerves. But he couldn't imagine having a drink under any circumstances. Instead, he got into his car and drove to Lighthouse Beach.

When he reached the beach, he removed his shoes and rolled up his pants so he could walk along the edge of the surf, allowing the warm tidal water to wash over his bare feet. Key West lay straight south beyond San Carlos Bay, deep in the dazzling glow of the Gulf of Mexico. There had been a lighthouse here since 1884, warning sailors away from the sandbars lurking offshore. Funny about that date. He seemed to have known it all his life as, in a sense, he had known Sanibel and Captiva.

His mother and two aunts used to bring Tree, his brother, Jimmy, and their three cousins to Sanibel Island for two weeks each January. The aunts piled the kids into a big green Desoto Adventurer that towed a little black trailer, and together they all set out for Florida.

In the years before it was linked by a causeway, the only way to reach Sanibel was via a ferry—one dollar per car, an additional thirty-five cents for each passenger—across from Punta Rasa on the mainland. The name meant flat point. In the very early days cattle had been shipped from there bound for Cuba.

Once on the island, they parked the trailer at the edge of whatever beach caught their fancy. Swimsuits were produced, tents for the kids pitched, sleeping bags unfurled, strict orders issued to have a good time. Those were days of gold and laughter, the only really happy days of his childhood.

Tree and Jimmy and the cousins would splash in the warm gulf waters overseen by a stern trio that kept one eye on their kids while at the same time devouring local resident Anne Murrow Lindbergh's *Gift from the Sea*. The book urged a state of inner spiritual grace. Tree's mother and her sisters loved that idea. They spent long hours enthusiastically discussing the remote yet hopeful possibility, their voices drifting across the sand as the cousins bobbed in and out of crystalline water. Tree always wondered if they had ever found the inner peace they sought, suspected they didn't, except perhaps during those warm winter days on Sanibel.

In the afternoons, wearing the sunhats they hated, the

boys were required to accompany the aunts on shell-hunting expeditions at the beach on the Captiva side of Blind Pass.

At low tide, when the shelling was best, everyone adopted what was known as "the Sanibel Stoop" searching the mud-flats and sandbars just beneath the water's murky surface for the yellow-line buttercup, the multi-colored calico, the scalloped rose cockle, the curiously marked Chinese alphabet, the slender polished olive—three thousand varieties of shells, the tourist brochures boasted. Not the children's favorite pastime but they went along because the moms loved it.

They were saved from shelling one year by the arrival of a suitor for Tree's Aunt Shirley. Gaspar Leon was a local fishing guide named, he said, after the legendary pirate José Gaspar who made his headquarters at Sanibel Island. The women he captured during his buccaneering rampages were held prisoner on an adjacent island—how Captiva got its name.

According to local legend, José Gaspar buried stolen treasure on various islands, inspiring Gaspar Leon to take the kids treasure-hunting, occasionally interrupted by fishing expeditions in search of the sharp and tarpon and grouper that were plentiful in the shallow waters of Pine Island Sound. They never found treasure, but they caught plenty of fish.

At dusk the aunts grilled grouper and tarpon on the beach while Gaspar poured the ladies generous portions of Cuban rum. Around the campfire, everyone's belly full, the gentle Florida night falling, the sea calm, Gaspar spun dark tales of decimated Calusa Indians who inhabited the area and once ruled an empire, runaway slaves, vicious slave catchers, and poachers. In the early 1900s, the poachers nearly wiped out the Florida egrets in their lust for the colorful plumes that were all the fashion rage. He recalled hurricanes that created islands, redfish so thick they turned the waters crimson, tarpon so plentiful they once fueled the local economy. He would drink rum and talk, lamenting the folly of man, so willing to destroy the natural things around him.

Men were varmints, Gaspar said. You could trust the osprey and you could trust the redfish. But the two things on this island you could never trust were alligators and man. Came down to it, Gaspar would take an alligator any day over a man. At least you knew what you were getting into with a gator. You never knew with a man.

Nights like that could go on forever as far as Tree was concerned. Life like this could go on forever too. What happened? Tree wasn't certain. Perhaps they just got older or the sisters drew apart or life simply flew away in other directions. He couldn't even remember when they stopped coming, but stop they did. Sanibel winters were no more.

Except in fond memory—until many years later when Freddie met Ray Dayton at the storied Broadmoor Hotel in Colorado Springs while attending the annual Grocery Manufacturers Association conference. They ended up seated together during the president's dinner. He offered her a job running his five supermarkets headquartered at a place in Florida called Sanibel Island.

Dayton's Supermarkets were doing okay, but the competition was starting to hurt. Ray had a sense the world was passing him by. He wanted to change, expand. Freddie could help him do that. Not that he ever expected her to take him up on his offer. It was a joke—glamorous big city woman comes to a little business on a faraway island, working for a dictatorial old fart who has yet to be dragged kicking and screaming into the twenty-first century. What were the chances of that happening?

But Freddie, as much to her surprise as Mr. Ray's, was intrigued. She came home to tell Tree about the offer, not expecting him to know where Sanibel even was. He laughed when he heard this. He knew where it was, all right. Yes, he knew—head due south and turn right at the sun. Sanibel lay straight ahead out there in the mist of his childhood, a dream shaped like the palm of a hand floating in the Gulf of Mexico. The long finger north of the palm? Captiva Island, where José Gaspar used to hold his female captives, a place Freddie found even more intriguing than Sanibel.

Even so, Tree did not think she would do it. He would move in an instant, fed up with Chicago and its imbedded memories of a newspaper life that could never be again. But Freddie had a career. He could not imagine her giving it up even for the undeniable lure of Sanibel-Captiva.

She probably wouldn't have either if not for the dolphins. They rented a motorboat and had lunch on nearby Useppa Island at the old Collier Inn. The CIA had once used the inn as a headquarters from which to train the Bay of Pigs invaders. It stood at the end of a romantic walkway with blooming cereus twisting around live oak and Spanish moss hanging from dramatically spreading Banyan trees.

After lunch they headed back across Pine Island Sound in their rented motorboat. Just past Cabbage Key, Tree cut the engine. On a whim, they stripped off their clothes and dived into the warm blue water.

They were splashing around together when darting grey forms approached, slipping just beneath the surface. Freddie screamed in alarm, thinking for one blind moment they were being attacked by sharks. Then one of the creatures soared gracefully out of the water before disappearing again. Not sharks, dolphins. They leapt and dived playfully around the two swimmers, nuzzling against them before swishing away, only to reappear again. Tree and Freddie spent the rest of that perfect, windless afternoon with the dolphins of Pine Island Sound. Freddie was converted. Chicago could not compete with dolphins.

———

Standing there on Lighthouse Beach, Tree thought of a piece of doggerel his Aunt Shirley used to recite during their winter visits.

The misty memory of a world
Where struggle is, and scars
Floats by us like a shadow.
And is lost among the stars.

Maybe not so lost, after all. *Stay away from her.* Who was he supposed to stay away from? The woman who had broken Reno's heart? Who was that? Must have been a mistake, except Reno O'Hara didn't strike Tree as the kind of guy who made too many mistakes about this sort of thing. He wondered if he should go to the police. Did private detectives go to the police? Seemed like he might be breaking the private detective code or something.

His cell phone buzzed. He fumbled for it in his pants pocket, coming away from the shore as he opened it up.

"I phoned your office." Freddie.

"I was just thinking about you," he said.

"Where are you?"

"On a case," he said.

"Come on."

"If you must know, I'm at the beach."

That brought silence. Then: "Are you all right?"

"Why wouldn't I be?"

"You're at the beach at eleven o'clock in the morning."

"Maybe I go to the beach more often than you think," he said. "Maybe there are all sorts of things about me you don't know. It could be I'm an international man of mystery who has been leading a double life all these years."

A telling beat ensued before she said, "Okay. What time are you going to be home?"

Tree turned and started back for the parking lot. He saw a young figure who he recognized after a moment as Marcello, the kid from his office. Still wearing the baseball cap and khaki shorts, he stood astride a bright red bike. Its frame gleamed in the sunlight, a boy's dream of a bike.

"Let me call you back, honey," he said.

"Sure you're okay?"

"I'm fine."

Tree closed his cell phone. Marcello squinted up at him, all but lost in his Sanibel Island T-shirt. The backpack hung from his shoulders.

"I followed you here," Marcello said. He nodded at his bicycle. "On my bike."

"Maybe you should be the detective," Tree said. "Did you find your mother okay?"

"No."

"I'm sorry to hear that," Tree said.

"I've got another card though. Want to see it?"

"Sure."

Marcello extracted from his backpack the same sort of blue greeting card he had shown Tree in the office. He took it from Marcello's outstretched hand, and held it at arm's length, squinting, trying to read the writing.

"You should wear your glasses," Marcello said.

"They're just for reading," Tree said.

"Right."

Tree got his glasses out and put them on and then studied the card: more of the neat handwriting he saw before. He read aloud:

"'Hi, my little love. Won't be long now. I can't wait to see you. I'm looking forward to going to the beach with you. Hope you still like to swim. I know I certainly do. There are dolphins out in Pine Island Sound. We can go swimming with them. How does that sound? It won't be long, I promise. In the meantime, stay brave and never forget how much I love you. Mommy.'"

Tree handed the card back to Marcello and removed his glasses. "That's very nice. How do you get these letters?"

Marcello looked irritated. "How do you think I get them? They come in the mail."

"Do you still have the envelopes they came in?"

"They didn't give me no envelopes," Marcello said.

"Who didn't give them to you? Your stepparents?"

"I've been thinking," Marcello said. "I should pay. You know, money."

He reached into his pocket and withdrew a crumpled wad of one dollar bills and thrust them at Tree. "Here," he said. "There's seven dollars."

"Seven dollars."

"Not enough?" The boy looked defiant, arm outstretched, the money gripped in his fist.

"That's not the point," Tree said. "The point is, you should be going to the police with something like this."

"I don't want the police." Marcello's voice was adamant. "I don't like the police. They're no good. That's why I'm paying you. So's I don't have to go to the police."

Tree sighed. "Keep your money," he said.

"No." The boy's hand shook. "I want you to take the money. Then we have a deal. That's the way it's done. We make a deal. You work for me."

Tree took the bills out of the boy's fist. Maybe he could redeem himself a bit. "When's the last time you saw your mom?"

"A long time ago," Marcello said. "When I was little."

"Do you remember what she looked like?"

"She was pretty."

"But you haven't seen her recently?"

Marcello shook his head.

"Just the letters."

"That's right."

Tree stared down at the mash of one dollar bills. His first payday. He looked at Marcello. "Where do you live?"

"What difference does that make?"

"Listen, if I'm going to help you find your mom, I need you to be a little more cooperative."

"Cooperative." Marcello repeated the word as though he had never heard it before.

"What's your mom's name?"

"Mom."

Tree stared at him. Marcello looked defiant. "Well, it is."

"That's all? You don't even know your mom's name?"

"If I knew my mom's name I wouldn't need you to find her, would I?"

There was a certain undeniable logic to that, Tree thought.

"And I don't have no more money," added Marcello.

An Irish guy named O'Hara had threatened him first thing this morning, and now a black kid named Marcello, a client by any definition, had paid him money. Maybe he was a real detective after all. Okay, detective, he thought. How do you go about finding a kid's mother?

His eyes fell on the red bicycle. "Is that new?"

5

I thought you only wore your glasses reading," Marcello said, seated beside Tree in the Beetle.

"I only need them for reading," Tree said.

"Then how come you have them on now?"

"I have to read traffic signs."

"This is a really crummy car," Marcello said.

"It's a Volkswagen," Tree said. "The Beetle. My pride and joy. The only thing I own in this life."

"I hate this car," Marcello said. They rode in silence for a couple of minutes. Marcello looked over at him. "This is all you own?"

"Well, how much do you own?"

"I'm just a kid," Marcello said. "When I grow up I'm gonna be rich."

"That's great news," Tree said. "How are you going to do that?"

"Not gonna tell."

"Just as well," Tree said. "I might steal your idea and become rich myself."

"That's the truth," Marcello said. "How come you're all grown up and you're so poor?"

"I ask myself that all the time."

"Don't you own a house?"

"Belongs to my wife," Tree said. "I'm lucky to have a roof over my head."

"You got no money, what kind of detective are you?"

"The kind that's willing to help you for seven bucks," Tree said.

That silenced Marcello. Tree drove onto Periwinkle Way and turned into Fennimore's Cycle Shop.

"Do you want to come in or wait here?"

"I'll wait here."

Tree wheeled the bike into the interior of the shop. He wound his way through rows of bike racks until he encountered a heavyset woman in a stripped T-shirt and jeans. Her left arm was etched in dragon tattoos.

She said, "Your wife works over at Dayton's, doesn't she?"

"That's right," Tree said. "Freddie's running the place."

"Ray Dayton runs the place."

"That's what Freddie keeps telling me." Tree smiled disarmingly. That is if sixty-year-old males could still smile disarmingly. "But I'm such a blind fan of my wife that I just can't believe she's not in charge."

The woman chuckled. "I hear you're a detective. That true?"

Tree held out his hand. "Tree Callister. "

She took his hand. "Molly Lightower." She held up her arm.

"They call me the Dragon Lady."

"Because of *Terry and the Pirates*?"

"Because I'm festooned with dragons, baby. Head to foot. Places I can't show you without being arrested."

"I see."

"I used to run with Hell's Angels in Cincinnati," she said.

"Are there Hell's Angels in Cincinnati?"

"My first old man was a sergeant at arms for the local chapter." She held up her right arm. Angel wings framed the letters AFFA. "That stands for angels forever, forever angels."

"Is there a Hell's Angels chapter on Sanibel Island?"

"Are you kidding? That was my dark past, honey, I'm a good girl now."

"Sorry to hear it," Tree said.

"Yeah, some days I am, too." She looked at the bike. "What can I do you for? You out detecting or what?"

"I'm trying to find out who bought this bike."

"The Electra Townie."

"Is that what it is?"

"Twenty-one speeds. More bike than you need around here, but that's what the kids want. Also, there are linear pull brakes on both wheels. Makes stopping easier. That's what parents like—and the saddle's easy on the bum thanks to the elastomers."

"Did you sell the bike?"

"Me? I didn't, no. But then I've been away for the past week. Up in Tampa. Mother's appendix burst of all things. Ninety-years-old and her appendix goes. She hates my tattoos. Russ probably sold it."

"Is Russ in?"

"My man Russ. Saved me from myself, that boy did. Tamed a Hell's Angels mama. Today, he's not in. But it would be in the computer."

"Would you mind looking it up?"

"How's your wife get along with that bugger Ray?"

"Pretty well I think," Tree said. "They talked for a long time before Freddie came to work for him so they both knew what to expect from each other. So far they've managed to co-exist pretty well."

"I've known that old bastard for thirty years. He was in Nam, you know."

"So I hear," Tree said.

"Those Nam guys, who knows how screwed up they got over there. Drugs, Agent Orange, booze, clap. No end to the way they could mess themselves up."

She was moving toward the desktop PC on the counter.

"Let's see." She put on a pair of glasses and clicked away

at the keyboard. "Yeah. Here it is. Russ sold it last week. Red Electra Townie."

"That's the one."

"Jeez," Molly said, "four hundred eighty bucks. That's practically our most expensive bike, at least for kids. Hold on." Her fingers clacked against more keys. "Okay. The bike was sold to a woman named Dara Rait. She paid by credit card. Visa. The address is off-island, interestingly enough. Seven hundred sixty San Carlos Blvd."

Tree wrote the address down on the back of a hydro bill he found in his back pocket "I appreciate this."

"I helped with your detecting?"

"You certainly did."

"Hope you can make a living at this detecting business," she said. "Because you know what?"

"What's that, Molly?"

"I don't think your wife is going to last long with our Mr. Ray as he likes to be called. No one does."

"No?"

"He's a mean old Nam vet. Lot of crazies were over there. In Nam, I mean. I knew some. He's one of them."

"Then I'd better get to work, hadn't I?"

"Good luck, honey," Molly said.

Tree rolled the bike out to the car. Marcello wasn't inside. He had disappeared.

"You little bastard," he said out loud. Then he was sorry he said it. Maybe something scared the kid. Or worse, maybe someone took him away.

He stood beside the Beetle for a few minutes in case the boy returned. He didn't. He put the bike in the back seat and then pulled the hydro bill out of his pocket and stared at the address he'd written down. He stood there, trying to figure out what to do next.

What the hell, he thought.

———

Along San Carlos Boulevard, closer to Fort Myers Beach,

the theme was distinctly nautical—the Mariner's Hotel, a crab shack called Pincer's, storefronts full of bikinis and beach balls. He swung right just before the Matanzas Pass Bridge, turning onto Main Street and then another right onto San Carlos Drive.

A stern sign warned the Bon Air Motor Court was private property, and there was no trespassing. Tree parked on the shoulder of the road. Number 760 stood at the intersection of San Carlos and a gravel road going off into the motor court. A knot of residents gossiped at the far end of the road near the water. Further along San Carlos Drive, workmen moved construction machinery aimlessly around, pretending to repair the road.

A white-painted motor home stood under impressive oaks. Rusty lawn furniture was scattered in front of a faded lattice-work barrier. The ornate face on a hanging clock said 2:20. A narrow, parched garden, marked off by white-painted stones, ran along either side of rickety aluminum steps leading up to a peeling screen door. Tree could hear the sound of a TV. Riotous laughter followed by delighted applause.

Tree knocked on the door. The sound of the television abruptly stopped. Tree thought he could hear movement inside. He knocked again, rattling the glass panel of the door. A short-haired black woman appeared and launched a fight with the screen door. The door finally gave up and popped open.

"Hey there, brother," she said. "What can I do for you?"

"I'm looking for Dara Rait."

The woman eased the door open wider. She wore a brown pantsuit, the jacket open to reveal a cream-colored blouse. "Are you now? Who shall I say is calling?"

"Are you Dara?"

"Supposing I am. Who are you?"

"My name is Tree Callister."

"And why would an individual named Tree Callister be looking for her?"

"Are you Dara or not?"

"Brother, I asked what you might be doing looking for Dara."

"I'd like to talk to her."

"And supposing Dara doesn't want to talk to you?"

"I've got information about a boy named Marcello," Tree said.

"Who is this Marcello?"

"Maybe her son."

"Her son?"

"That's right."

"You sure Dara has a son?"

"That's what I'm trying to find out. Who are you?" Tree said "Are you a friend of Dara's?"

"I'm no friend, but I do know her," the woman said, producing a badge. The badge said Sanibel-Captiva Police.

6

The police officer drew Tree into the gloom of the motor home. He half expected to see a dead body lying on the floor. But there was no body among the clothes strewn everywhere.

The police officer said her name was Cee Jay Boone. "It's not the initials, though."

She spelled it out for him. "C-e-e. J-a-y. Detective Cee Jay Boone."

"I didn't know Sanibel-Captiva had a detective."

"In fact there's two of us. So now you know who I am, and you know a little something about the workings of my department. So brother, remind me again of your name."

"It's Callister. Tree Callister."

"That's right, Tree. What are you doing here, Tree?"

"I'm a private detective."

"Are you now? I didn't know they had a private dick on Sanibel Island."

"They've only got one as far as I know," Tree said.

"And you're it."

"Don't sound so disappointed."

"Well, you know, Tree, you could have worn a trench coat or something."

"It's too hot. When it's cooler, I wear the trench coat."

"Okay, Tree Callister, private detective. You're looking for Dara because you think she has a son named Marcello."

"That's right."

Tree told her about Marcello and how he had tracked Dara to this address. Cee Jay listened to him without comment and then asked, "This Marcello, what's his last name?"

"I don't know."

"So then where does he live?"

"Maybe he lives here."

"Here?" Cee Jay looked around at the mess of the place. Then her gaze returned to Tree. "I don't get it. Who's paying you to help this kid?"

"Marcello's paying," Tree said.

"A twelve-year-old boy hired you?"

"That's correct," Tree said.

"How much is he paying you?"

Tree paused before he said, "Seven dollars."

She stared at him. "Seven dollars?"

"It's a retainer," Tree said.

"What are you?" she said. "Some kind of idiot?"

"Just a guy who works cheap."

"Boy, you sure do," Cee Jay said.

The door opened and a squat man stepped inside, mopping his perspiring forehead with a white handkerchief. His hair was cut close to his bullet head, making him look like a wrestler at a job interview. He wore a badly fitting blue sports jacket and a white golf shirt.

"Come on in, Mel," Cee Jay said. "Join the party."

"I checked around the park," the man named Mel said. "Nobody's seen her for at least a week."

He looked Tree up and down.

"This is Tree Callister," Cee Jay said. "Tree here is a detective. Tree, this is my partner, Detective Mel Scott."

"A detective, huh?" Mel looked right through him. "What kind of detective?"

"The private kind," said Cee Jay "You got six bucks? You can hire Tree. He works cheap."

"Seven," Tree corrected. "Seven dollars."

"The cheap detective." Mel issued a snort of laughter then turned to Cee Jay. "She's taken a powder. So let's get back to the office."

"Why? What's Dara done?" Tree asked.

"It's not what Dara's done," Cee Jay said. "It's her friend Reno O'Hara. That's who we're looking for. Can you help us out, Tree?"

In an attempt to redeem himself somewhat in Detective Boone's eyes, Tree told her that he'd encountered Reno O'Hara that morning. Mel listened, cocking his head in Tree's direction as though not sure he was hearing correctly. He kept his eyes on Cee Jay.

"Why would Reno O'Hara want to see you?" Mel asked.

"He said he was looking for someone. He thought I knew where this person was."

"Did someone have a name?"

"No."

Mel said, "So Reno thought you knew someone. Only you didn't know anyone."

"Could be he thought I know Dara Rait."

"Except you don't," said Cee Jay Boone.

"No, I don't."

"But Tree, here you are, looking for Dara Rait."

"I'm looking for a boy's mother."

"Oh, yeah," Cee Jay said. "The kid who paid you seven dollars."

"Here's the thing," Mel Scott said. "Doesn't make any difference who you know or don't know. You got Reno O'Hara on your tail, you are one sorry dude."

Cee Jay nodded agreement. "If you're on Reno's radar screen, brother, you better hope we find him sooner than later."

"What's he done?" Tree asked.

Cee Jay and Mel traded glances. Cee Jay said, "That's police business. It's not private detective business."

7

"You haven't seen my glasses have you?"

"Why don't you put them in the same place every time and then you won't lose them." Freddie brushed pesto on fresh grouper.

"I do put them in the same place, except I forget where that place is."

"The last time I saw them, they were on the kitchen counter."

"I would not have left them on the counter, I can tell you that much."

Tree disappeared into the house. She put the filets on the barbecue, and then stepped back into the house. She encountered Tree wearing his glasses.

"Where were they?"

"On the kitchen counter."

Tree watched the fish on the barbecue while Freddie fixed a salad with baby arugula and small tomatoes.

Once the fish was done, she added oil and vinegar to the salad and they sat on the terrace watching the sun set while Freddie recounted the events of her day: the continuing attempts to update the computer system, a general manager who said he could deliver but didn't, her efforts to persuade Ray to adapt a realistic planning strategy for the coming year. Sometimes, she said, she felt as though she was speaking to him in a foreign language. Then it was Tree's turn. He told Freddie about Reno O'Hara, Marcello on the beach, the bike shop, and the boy's subsequent disappearance. He told her about the Bon Air Motor Park and the police. He did not say the police thought Reno O'Hara highly dangerous and capable of killing Tree. That was not a conversation over chardonnay and sunsets on the terrace.

Even so, by the time Tree finished, Freddie was sitting up, calm as always, but more intense than usual. She put her plate to one side without finishing the grouper.

"Not to sound like the concerned wife or anything."

"Of course not."

"But are you sure you know what you're getting yourself into?"

"I don't have a clue. A guy named Reno O'Hara shows up at the office looking for a woman. I have no idea who she is. But he doesn't believe me."

"Okay, I'm following you so far," Freddie said.

"Then I end up at a trailer park looking for a woman named Dara Rait. That's when the police showed up."

"What were the police doing there?"

"Looking for Reno O'Hara."

"Why?"

"They won't say. But they do say that Dara Rait is mixed up with him."

"So you're thinking Dara is the woman Reno came to your office looking for."

"He must have followed Marcello."

"Who is looking for his mother. Dara?"

"I don't know. The police don't seem to think Dara has a son. Marcello disappeared before I had a chance to ask him."

"What did they think of you showing up in the midst of all this?"

"The two detectives gave me the distinct impression they think I'm an idiot."

"Not an idiot," Freddie said. "Maybe just a nice guy in over his head."

———

Tree was back in a newspaper city room, desperate to finish a story. What story? He couldn't remember. The big wall clock ticked loudly. Smoke curled in the air. White men in white shirts jabbed at typewriter keys so fast their fingers blurred. The sound was deafening. He couldn't find a place to work, and he still could not remember what story he was supposed to write. If he did not produce a story he would lose his job. He couldn't lose it. The job was all he had. It defined who he was. Without it, he wasn't anything.

Tree jerked awake in the dark. It took a few moments to realize he was no longer at the newspaper; there was no need to worry about stories or deadlines. He looked over to where Freddie slept, her back to him, a reassuring presence in the darkness.

He sat on the edge of the bed taking deep breaths. He heard a noise from the other room. Visions of Reno O'Hara breaking into the house assailed him.

Get a grip, he told himself. Newspaper deadlines did not loom. Bad guys were not invading. They were safe.

He knew this time of night; the hours of nightmares and demons and endless uncertainty. Gloom floated, death was close.

Had he heard something?

He rose from the bed and slipped across to the bedroom door. He peered out through the shadows occupying the house at this hour. Nothing moved. All was quiet.

"My love," Freddie called. "Come back to bed. It's all right."

And maybe it was.

8

Happy tourists filled the visitors center the next morning. There was no sign of threatening evil in the person of Reno O'Hara—good news for Sanibel tourism, better news for Tree. Feeling more relaxed, he got himself a cup of coffee and then leaned against the counter trading pleasantries with the trio of volunteers on duty.

Rex Baxter came down from his office, brightening as soon as he saw the reception area full of visitors. "Anyone here from Chicago?"

One of the tourists recognized him from his weatherman days. Pleased, Rex soon was holding court. "I'm not from Chicago originally," he said. "I was born on the Oklahoma panhandle. The panhandle's so flat you can watch your dog run away for two days."

The group exploded in laughter.

"People always ask me why I left Chicago," Rex continued. "I always tell 'em it's because the weather is so easy to forecast down here. You just paste a smile on your face and say, 'Sunny.'"

Someone asked if he knew Barack Obama in Chicago. Rex got that question all the time, and he didn't like it. He had left town by the time the future president came along. "I knew Mayor Daley, though. Mayor Daley said I was his favorite weatherman."

"That's the current mayor?" the visitor from Chicago said.

"No, no, his old man," Rex said.

The Chicago visitor looked blank-faced.

"What you want to do," Rex went on, relieved to change the subject, "you want to get over to the Ding Darling Wildlife Refuge. That's where we got the replica of the biggest darn gun you ever laid eyes on."

"What are you doing with a gun over there?" someone wanted to know.

"Ding Darling was a world famous cartoonist, a household word. I grew up reading his stuff at a time when editorial cartoonists still had real influence, him more than most. He was also a pioneering conservationist who did more than just about anyone to get the wetlands around here protected."

"Ding owned a gun?" One of the visitors sounded nonplused.

"No, no. It wasn't Ding's gun, but he had it hanging on the wall in his office. Blunderbuss of a thing, used by Maryland poachers in the 1930s. The poachers filled the rifle full of buckshot, aimed it at a flock of ducks and pulled the trigger. *Blam! Blam!* Killed dozens of birds with a single shot, an environmental travesty, of course, the sort of thing Ding Darling fought against his whole life."

Scattered applause warmed Rex to his subject.

"What me and a couple of buddies have done, we've built a replica of the gun, trigger mechanism, the whole thing."

"You can shoot this mother?" The question came from a tourist displaying a large belly beneath a red golf shirt.

"You bet," said Rex. "We got her loaded up with buckshot. You folks are around Saturday, come on over to Ding Darling's. We'll be giving demonstrations, aiming it at targets we got set up. It's something to see, I promise you."

An excited murmur was followed by assurances from his eager audience that they would be there. Rex pumped hands and slapped backs before making his way over to where Tree was finishing his coffee.

"You should go over and have a look at that gun, Tree."

"I will, Rex."

"It's something else."

They stood looking at one another.

"What, Rex?"

"That woman."

"What woman?"

"The one upstairs in your office."

"There's a woman in my office?"

"Wasn't sure you knew."

"Rex, for God's sake. You should have said something before now."

"Didn't know what to think of some babe who wasn't Freddie in your office."

"Babe?"

"She's a bit of a babe, yeah."

"You might think she was a client, Rex. That might have crossed your mind. I am a detective, after all."

Rex looked at him as though he was crazy.

Tree hurried up the stairs. The woman sat in the visitor's chair. As soon as he saw her, he knew who she was. He'd seen her photograph in the papers often enough. She wore a white dress with a scooped neckline and a flared skirt that showed off long tanned legs.

"The door was open so I walked in," she said in a throaty voice. Exactly the voice Tree would have imagined.

He squeezed past her to his desk.

In the detective fiction he read as a kid, the femme fatale appeared at the detective's office in chapter one. She kept crossing and uncrossing long legs. The thought of female legs crossing gave Tree a frisson of adolescent lust. This wasn't exactly the first chapter of Tree's life. Nothing about his life, or anyone else's, ever fell into anything as neat as a chapter. He was no longer certain of lustful frissons either, or whether there were such things as femmes fatale, only stupid men. But if there were, the woman seated in front of him certainly would qualify.

She said, "I wasn't sure if I had the right address. I always thought this was the Chamber of Commerce."

"It is," he said. "But they let me have an office here."

The woman glanced around. "The Sanibel Sunset Detective Agency?"

"I'm the Sanibel Sunset detective."

"There's only one of you?" Surprise marred the perfect symmetry of her face.

"I bring in associates when needed," Tree lied.

"I was driving by. Well, I drive by here a good deal. I'm up at Captiva." She spoke in a flat, slightly accented drawl, mid-Atlantic. A voice that had spent more time in Europe than it had "up at Captiva."

"I saw your ad in the local paper." She shrugged. "I don't know. I've never hired a private detective before. I'm not at all sure how it's done."

"Why don't you tell me what the problem is, and then we can take it from there," Tree said in his most reassuring voice. It went nicely with his sympathetic face.

"Now it sounds as though I'm seeing a therapist." The hint of a smile. Tree smiled back.

"I should probably tell you my name. That would help."

"It would," Tree agreed.

She took a deep breath. "My name is Elizabeth Traven." She looked at him expectantly. "Traven. Does that name mean anything to you?"

"You're Brand Traven's wife. The media mogul."

"Media mogul," she repeated. "Sounds funny, like a comic book hero. Media Mogul."

"Media Mogul is in jail."

"A federal prison," Elizabeth Traven corrected. "The Coleman Federal Correctional Complex."

"That's a maximum security facility, isn't it?"

"There's a minimum security wing where Brand is housed. I mean it's prison. Maximum. Minimum. Whatever. It's still prison."

"A fraud conviction."

"They accused him of defrauding his company. But they actually convicted him on a single charge. Obstruction of justice. Nonsense. Because he moved a few boxes."

Tree aimed a sympathetic nod in her direction, remembering the boxes contained evidence pertaining to the case. The removal had been caught on a security camera.

"How's he doing up there?"

"Brand is doing fine. Brand always does fine. No matter what. That's Brand. He adjusts to his circumstances. He survives. That's what he does."

A fleeting, uncertain look was followed by silence. She crossed and uncrossed her legs. Tree tried not to look. Elizabeth Traven cleared her throat.

"We've lived in New York and London for the past twenty years or so. Captiva is our winter retreat. But ever since Brand's been at Coleman, I've stayed here, driving to see him three or four times a week. You spend a lot of time waiting at Coleman, in a kind of holding room where they put inmate wives and girlfriends, lawyers too, but mostly it's the women. It becomes sort of a bonding thing. You spend so much time there. In a way, we all become inmates."

She glanced out the window, as though the rest of her story might be in the parking lot.

"I've become friends with a woman whose husband is a dealer in stolen goods, at least that's what she says. He's serving time for manslaughter, which means he killed someone but didn't do it intentionally. According to my friend, her husband never killed anyone unintentionally. So there you go, Mr. Callister, these are the kind of people you get involved with when your husband ends up in prison; the criminal class. I suppose in your line of work, you are used to such types."

Tree nodded solemnly, as though intimately familiar with the criminal class.

"Well, for me, it's alien territory, let me assure you. But I like Michelle. Something rather captivating about her. Fascinating."

"Michelle?"

"Michelle Crowley."

Tree put on his glasses and made a note. Elizabeth Traven said, "You wear glasses?"

"Just for reading."

"Everyone calls her Mickey. Hispanic mother who was a drug addict. Black father doing life in Idaho or some such place. A brother was killed in a drive-by shooting. Stories of growing up in the Overtown section of Miami that are not to be believed."

"She lives around here now?"

"Fort Myers. She had to take the bus to Coleman, which isn't easy, so I drove her back and forth on the days when I visited. It was nice to have the company. You've got nothing in common, really, but in fact for the moment you've got everything.

"A few times we ended up eating together because it was late after the drive back, and neither of us felt like cooking. Then she began calling me—late at night, first thing in the morning.

"After that, she would show up at odd hours. I'd drive to the supermarket or walk on the beach, and she'd follow me."

She paused and looked at him. Tree threw his glasses on the desk. "It sounds as though there might be reason for concern."

She re-crossed her legs. He fought off memories of the bad women who filled the paperback detective novels of his youth.

"So that's where we are at the moment," Elizabeth said. "I find her actions threatening. I'm never sure when she's going to appear, and I'm not certain what she will do next. I don't want to go to the police because she hasn't done anything. Maybe she is just lonely and needs a friend and has gone a little overboard. I don't know."

"What can I do to help?" Tree was pleased with the way he phrased the question. It had a nice professional ring to it.

"You may or may not know, I'm a writer."

"A biography of Karl Marx."

Elizabeth looked pleasantly surprised. "Among others, yes. I'm trying to get a new book done. Trotsky. His life and times. He's giving me enough trouble. I don't need any more distractions. I'm feeling vulnerable, perhaps a little more frightened than I like to admit."

"Why don't I see what I can find out about this woman, ascertain what she's up to, what sort of threat she presents, and then get back to you. We can decide on next steps from there."

"What do you charge for this sort of thing, Mr. Callister?"

"Two hundred dollars a day, plus expenses."

The deal breaker. Would he pay two hundred dollars a day for his services? No. But Elizabeth Traven was made of stronger stuff. "How be I pay you for a week? Throw in one hundred dollars for expenses. Would that be enough?"

Tree's throat was dry. "I don't see why not."

She bent to pick up the plum-colored Gucci bag on the floor beside her. She opened the strap and withdrew a wad of one hundred dollar bills. Did the wives of jailed rich men carry their wealth around in Gucci bags? A little known fact about the rich in American life.

She counted out fifteen bills and laid them on the desk. Tree tried not to look at the money. Elizabeth Traven recrossed her legs and returned the purse to the floor.

"Would you like a receipt?"

"No. But there is one more thing." She studied him with pale eyes that Tree imagined might be able to see right through a person such as himself, a person trying to be one thing when he was something else entirely.

"What's that?"

"In addition to purchasing its services, I assume I am also buying Sanibel Sunset Detective's discretion?"

"You are, absolutely."

"This business between us must remain strictly confidential."

"That goes without saying," Tree said.

"Does it?" She sat up straight. "Well, just in case, now it's been said."

"I'm going to need whatever information you have on Mickey Crowley."

"Such as?"

"A photograph would help."

"I don't have one."

"Her address?"

"All I have is where I dropped her off. MacGregor Woods on Barrington Court."

"What about her husband's name?"

"It's Dwayne."

"Dwayne Crowley?"

"As far as I know, yes."

"What about a description of Mickey?"

"Let me see. African American. About five feet, three inches tall. Slim figure. Rather attractive, in a dusky sort of way. Short black hair. Yes, and she has some sort of tattoo on her shoulder. A rose, I think."

Tree retrieved his glasses from the desk and then spent some time writing down the information. "I'll need your phone number."

She rose to her feet. "I'm impressed you know about the Marx book."

"The crazy days in Vienna before Karl and his brothers got into comedy."

She aimed a level gaze at him.

"You've heard those jokes before," he said.

"Let's meet again next Wednesday, Mr. Callister. Here in your office. Hopefully, by then you will have some results."

He watched her leave. Or rather he watched her behind moving beneath the material of the dress. He shouldn't have been doing that, but he was a detective, after all. That's what detectives did. They watched things.

9

"Think about it," Rex Baxter said. "These are grown men wearing *tights*."

Friday nights Rex presided over Fun Friday, which consisted of a group of local business people and their spouses gathered at the Lighthouse bar for drinks and, depending on the mood, dinner. Tree bought Freddie a glass of chardonnay as he listened to Rex in conversation with Todd Jackson.

"And not just tights. These guys run around in capes and masks. Can you imagine what the reaction would be if you walked out in the street like that?"

"I like Batman," Todd said, sipping a Heineken. "And I liked the first *Spider-Man*. Didn't like the others, though."

Todd, polished a walnut brown, operated Sanibel Biohazard, "a crime scene clean-up company," as he described it, that did a thriving business in the Naples-Fort Myers area.

"Batman's a good example of what I'm talking about," Rex continued. "How does he even get into that outfit? It's skin tight, for God's sake. Try getting into a skin-tight jumpsuit some time. See how long it takes you."

"Somehow on the big screen it all makes sense," Todd said.

"Doesn't make any sense at all. You're a young guy, you're pissed off at the world, so you put on a pair of tights and a mask to fight crime? Come on. Try it. See how far you get."

"I don't fight crime," Todd said. "I clean it up."

"Not only does the public accept this nonsense, it flocks to movie theaters to see it. These movies aren't just popular, they are phenomenal hits all over the world. I don't get it, I really don't."

"That's why all these movies are set in big Northeast cities," Todd said. "Can you imagine your average superhero in tights and a mask down here? Too hot. He'd have to wear a bathing suit."

The electric keyboard player crooned "My Heart Will Go On." Freddie nudged Tree. "Who can resist?"

"Not me," Tree said.

She put her drink on the bar and led him onto the dance floor. Tree told her about his encounter with Elizabeth Traven.

"Elizabeth Traven came to see you?"

"That's what I'm telling you."

"This afternoon?"

"This morning, first thing, actually."

Freddie shifted against him. He held her close.

"No comment?" Tree said.

"She's a hottie."

"A hottie?" His mind flashed to a view of Elizabeth Traven's legs. "She's too old to be a hottie."

"Tree, she's still a hottie." Freddie, adamant.

"She wrote a book on Marx. The philosopher. Not one of the brothers."

"Stalin, too. She's very anti-communist."

"She's doing Trotsky. One of my favorite communists."

"Her books are doorstoppers," Freddie said. "I'm surprised she has the time, what with her interestingly checkered past."

"We all have one of those."

"An interestingly checkered past? Not me."

"Two ex-husbands? That's checkered."

"Just seems boring to me."

"Maybe that's how Elizabeth sees her life," Tree said.

"The rumors about Bill Clinton?"

"There are rumors about Bill Clinton and everyone."

"Not about Bill and me," Freddie said.

"One of the reasons I married you," he said. "Everyone else was sleeping with Bill Clinton."

"Either that or you had already married them."

"Ha. Ha," Tree said.

Across the bar, Ray Dayton let out a victorious whoop. A helmeted gladiator on the big screen TV had won his approval. Mr. Ray didn't attend Fun Friday every week but when he did, he dragged Freddie along. She insisted Tree be present for moral support—and also to provide the escape route when the combination of beer and sports took their toll on her boss.

The song ended. They moved off the dance floor. Freddie said, "I hate to say something cliché like, 'Are you sure you know what you're doing?'"

"But?"

"Are you sure you know what you're doing?"

Tree had been wondering the same thing but he didn't like to admit it to Freddie. You could say you were a detective all you wanted, but actually being a detective with a client, well, that was something else.

"To me this sounds like another situation where the person ought to go to the police," Freddie continued.

"Elizabeth Traven should go to the police?"

"Don't you think so?"

"She shouldn't have come to me?"

"Let me put this as gently as possible: why would she come to you?"

"She saw my ad. She said she was driving past and decided to stop. On a whim."

"For which she paid fifteen hundred dollars in advance."

"Small change as far as she's concerned," Tree said.

Freddie didn't respond.

"I can do this," Tree said, as much to convince himself as Freddie.

"Can you?"

"Supposing she goes to the police. What does she tell them? 'This woman has done nothing to me, but I'm nervous and suspicious.' The police aren't going to do anything. They can't."

"Okay, the police can't do anything. What can you do?"

"Something," said Tree.

"Something doesn't sound like much of anything, Tree."

At the bar, Mr. Ray let out another whoop. Freddie squeezed Tree's hand and grimaced. "Lord, give me strength."

"Freddie, Freddie!" Ray's flushed face made the snowy white of his hair absolutely glow. Beside him, Rex Baxter, holding a Bud Lite, had stopped talking to Todd and focused on the TV. Ray slapped Todd on the shoulder as Freddie settled against the bar. "I want you to hear this guy. He talks just like you. Todd, tell her what you just told me. What are those initials?"

Todd grinned. "OPIM. Other Potentially Infectious Materials. Part of the service we offer. That way customers know we're not limited to crime scene stuff."

"Listen to him," Mr. Ray shouted. "Listen to this son of a bitch. That's what it is now. All these—what the hell do you call them?"

"Acronyms," Freddie said.

"Yeah, right. Give him your HMR, Freddie. Give him the damned gospel according to HMR."

Freddie rolled her eyes. "Home Meal Replacement. I'm trying to encourage Ray to expand our offering."

"I'll trade you one OPIM for two HMRs." He cackled with laughter.

The noise from the drinkers and diners all but drowned out the keyboard player's version of "Crackling Rosie." Ray threw his arm around Tree. "We haven't talked."

"Haven't we?"

"We should talk, Tree. You and me. The two of us, buddy."

Buddy? Tree thought.

Ray led Tree outside as the sun dropped into the gulf. Tree always marveled at the speed, as though it couldn't wait to get away. They went down a ramp to the dock. An emerging moon threw shadows across pleasure craft that never seemed to move. That was his problem, Tree reflected as the Ray Man guided him to a stop. He couldn't imagine owning a boat. How could he live in Florida thinking like that? He wasn't even interested in helmeted young men throwing footballs at one another. Something must be terribly wrong with him.

An electronically enhanced "Tie a Yellow Ribbon" disturbed the twilight. He glanced up at the windows along the porch, angry black eyes frowning down on him. He thought of Freddie peering out through one of those eyes, worried. Ray blew martini-scented breath at him. "Freddie's doing just fine."

"That's good to know," Tree said.

"I screw around, pretend I don't like all this new stuff she's bringing into the business—best practices, all that shit. But you know what, Tree? I love it, love what she's doing. Hauling me along. I'm kicking and screaming all the way, but she's getting me there, you know why?"

"Why Ray?"

"Because I'm no fool. The business is better for what's she doing and thanks to her, I'm gonna be richer than ever."

Tree grinned innanely and said, "That's great news, Ray."

The Ray Man tightened the pressure on Tree's shoulder. A sign of affection? Or an attempt to break his arm?

"But I've got to be honest with you, buddy. Do you mind if I'm honest?"

"I wouldn't want it any other way, Ray."

"Okay, good. I'm gonna lay it right out there. The one thing that worries me about all this is you."

"Me?" Tree couldn't help sounding surprised. Not that he didn't have a pretty good idea how the Ray Man felt about him.

"I mean, what is it with this private detective crap, anyway? What is that all about?"

Tree wasn't sure Ray wanted an answer, so he didn't try to give him one.

"Freddie tells me you used to be a pretty good newspaperman up north."

"I was in the newspaper business for a long time," Tree agreed.

"I mean those bastards really buggered up Vietnam, didn't they? Turned the country against our boys with their anti-war bullshit."

"That was so long ago, Ray. But I seem to recall Lyndon Johnson and Richard Nixon might have had something to do with it."

"So long ago, Tree? Guess it depends on your perspective, doesn't it? Not that I hold it against you, personally."

"That's a relief," Tree said.

"The important thing is, you had a career. You amounted to something. There was achievement."

"I don't know how much achievement was involved," Tree said.

"No, no. Don't put it down. A job. Career. That's good, a good thing. But this private eye stuff. I mean what is that all about, Tree? What is it all about?"

"It's what I do, Ray," Tree said.

"Gawd almighty, man. You're sixty years of age. You've got a beautiful, talented wife. And you're a freaking detective?"

"That's what I am, Ray."

"No, let me tell you what you are, Tree, and I'm gonna be brutally honest here because I've had a couple of drinks, okay?"

"Okay."

"You're a laughing stock, my friend. Okay? You're not a detective as far as most people around here are concerned. You're a laughing stock."

"Honey, it's time to go home."

Tree turned to find Freddie backlit by the light from the porch, standing at the bottom of the ramp. Ray gave up his claim on Tree's shoulder leaning forward, peering at Freddie, as though not certain who she was.

Freddie said, "Vera's inside, Ray." Vera was the Ray Man's long-suffering wife. Mrs. Ray, they called her. When things got bad enough on a Friday night, a phone call was made to Mrs. Ray.

"Tree and I were just having a little heart-to-heart," Ray said. "Man-to-man stuff. We're buddies, Tree and me. Right, Tree?"

Tree didn't say anything.

"It's time to go," Freddie said.

"Buddies. Okay? Tell her, Tree."

She took Tree's hand. "Good night, Ray."

"You're pissed off, and you shouldn't be."

"I'm not pissed," Freddie said.

"You are." Mr. Ray sounded hurt. "It's guy stuff, that's all."

They left him swaying on the dock in the descending gloom.

"I'm sorry about that." She squeezed his hand.

"It's all right."

"No, it's not."

"You know he could be right. Maybe I am a laughing stock."

"Not as far as I'm concerned."

He hugged her. "That's all that counts."

10

The swish of lawn sprinklers broke the morning silence in McGregor Woods. Handsome houses with terra cotta tile roofs set along gracefully curving roadways shimmered under an already-bright sun.

Tree parked around the corner from the Barrington Court address Elizabeth Traven had given him. A U.S. mail truck moved slowly from mail box to mail box, the driver leaning out the open door to deliver mail. An elderly woman in baggy jeans pulled at an excited Jack Russell.

Tree didn't play the radio fearing he would draw unwanted attention. He needn't have worried. The world was deserted. He occupied himself trying to imagine some sort of life behind the cool exteriors of the lovely McGregor Woods houses.

Imagination failed.

The night before he had googled Elizabeth Traven and her husband.

Brand Traven was as arrogant, intellectual, and gleefully controversial as Tree recalled. Elizabeth was the "tawny beauty," as one of the London tabloids described her, a bestselling author of revisionist biographies of Marx and Stalin. She had interviewed Brand for her Stalin book, although the Mayfair wags had a field day wondering what Traven would know about Stalin. It made no difference. Shortly after the interview, he left his wife of twenty-three years and moved in with Elizabeth.

With Elizabeth at his side, he was no longer merely the owner of newspapers and TV stations in the United States and Great Britain. Now he was part of a dynamic, attractive power couple, welcome in the world's best drawing rooms, friends with presidents, prime ministers, movie stars, Wall Street titans.

Members of the British Royal Family dropped by their Kensington digs. Mick Jagger strolled on the beach near their Captiva summer house. Wasn't that Bono with the couple in Paris? The rich and influential, dressed in bright costume, flocked to their Manhattan townhouse each winter for their annual Blue January fete. Elizabeth and Brand one year showed up as eighteenth century Medicis, Cosimo and his wife Marguerite. The humor! The charm! Endless.

Their extravagances were gleefully reported. The private jet sent to retrieve Elizabeth's fur coat because the she was cold in Florida (Cold in Florida? chorused the locals. Impossible). The renowned French chef flown to Tahiti to prepare dinner for two hundred nearest and dearest. The world's grandest yacht rented for a family vacation at a cost that would have funded an African country for a year.

In a simpler time none of this would have been questioned. Brand would have been all-powerful in the media world he created with hard work and personal sacrifice, the respect for his achievements undiminished, his authority unquestioned.

But the gods who decide these things decreed Brand Traven create his empire as the Internet exploded, putting into jeopardy the future of print and traditional broadcasting, canceling the licenses to print money that newspapers and television had traditionally represented. The global economic downturn, as Traven's own media called it, did not help matters.

Traven's inability to turn his empire around in the face of changing technology, his refusal to accommodate the new realities of doing business in a publicly held company, not to mention his increasingly opulent lifestyle, drew the ire of investors. Elizabeth and Brand partied on apparently oblivious as the empire wobbled, share price tumbled, and investors increasingly grumbled.

The end came when Brand was stripped of his corporate powers and charged with defrauding the very empire he created—stealing shareholders' money, they said. Brand loudly disagreed. It was his money. He had started the company, built it from virtually nothing before taking it public. How dare anyone question how he spent what he earned.

Ill-considered public statements about victimization at the hands of aggressive, politically motivated district attorneys followed, statements that set the public's teeth on edge and surely helped bring about the obstruction of justice conviction.

Brand was sentenced to seven years in prison. Not a bad outcome, given the time other CEOs were serving. Nonetheless, he launched appeals and wrote eloquently of the injustice of it all. To no avail. Once the rich were in jail, it became apparent, no one was particularly anxious to let them out again.

There was a great deal of speculation about the millions spent on high-powered lawyers. Not high-powered enough, apparently. The cost of defending himself, it was rumored, had drained off what little of Brand's fortune the feds could not confiscate.

Everyone wondered what Mrs. Traven was living on, holed up in her Captiva estate. Maybe the cash stuffed in her Gucci bag, Tree speculated.

———

The Jack Russell reappeared dragging the elderly woman. She brought the dog to a stop near Tree's car. He attempted to ignore her. She stood there inspecting him.

Tree smiled and nodded at her.

"Three hundred thousand," the woman said.

Tree said, "I beg your pardon?"

The woman led the dog over to the car. Pale, freckled skin was easily offended by Florida sun.

"Three hundred thousand. How much they're looking for on the short sale. That's what you're doing out here isn't it? Looking at the house, trying to figure out how much it's worth."

"Guess I gave it away, huh?" He tried to look sheepish— not hard under the circumstances.

"I don't know what happened to the sign," the woman continued. "Maybe kids took it. But that's what they want. A deal you ask me."

"If this is Michelle Crowley's place it certainly is," Tree said.

The woman frowned. "Michelle Crowley? No one named Michelle Crowley owns this place."

"No?"

"Far as I know it belongs to some lawyer in Orlando. He rents it out."

"Is it rented now?"

"I believe it is, although I haven't seen anyone around."

"Maybe I'll take a closer look," Tree said, getting out of the car. The Jack Russell tugged anxiously on his leash. "That three hundred thousand sounds like a pretty good price."

"You won't do better, not in this neighborhood. I keep a close eye on real estate prices around here. Sort of a hobby of mine. You can go over to Cape Coral and do better, but then you're sitting in a No Man's Land of unoccupied houses. Who knows when it's going to come back."

"Thanks," Tree said. "I appreciate your help."

"Come on, Mackenzie." The woman yanked at the dog. In response Mackenzie yapped loudly, and pulled even harder on his leash. "Dogs," the woman said. As though that explained everything.

Tree stood at the curb cursing himself. The great detective had spent hours watching an empty house.

He found an opening in a hedge and went through into a rectangular backyard with a swimming pool wrapped in a green sun dome screen to keep out insects.

A glass-topped table and four wrought iron chairs were on the terrace adjacent to the pool. The remnants of a candle dripped over a glass holder. A wrinkled *People* magazine on a chaise lounge lay open at "Lindsay Lohan's Beauty Secrets." Tree peered through sliding glass doors into a kitchen's shadowy dimness. He tried the latch. To his surprise, the door slid open.

Immediately, he was assailed by a sickly sweet scent. He stepped inside. The air was stifling. A granite countertop divided the kitchen from a family room. A fifty-two-inch Sony flat screen occupied a corner of the family room. There was no other furniture.

He made his way around the counter and saw something in the sink. He fished his glasses out of his breast pocket in order to get a clearer view of what he was looking at in the uncertain light. Sure enough, it was a human head. Tendrils of blond hair drifted against the backsplash.

Retreating along a short corridor, he entered a combination dining room and living room. A setting for six, with attractive pewter charger plates, was laid out on a mahogany table. A naked woman occupied a chair at the head of the table. It was difficult to see how she was going to eat since her head lay in the kitchen sink.

11

You look pretty shaken up," Cee Jay Boone said.

"Not me," Tree said. "I come across headless corpses two or three times a week."

"What? You've never seen a dead body before?" Detective Mel Scott's gravel voice dripped with disdain.

"My Uncle Morris when I was eight," Tree said. "He still had his head."

"A detective who can't look at dead people," Mel said. "Jeez. What will they think of next."

"Let me get this straight," said Cee Jay Boone. "You just happened to be driving past a house on Barrington Court and decided to have a look."

"Like I told you, detective," Tree said. "I heard there was a bank short sale. My wife and I have been thinking of moving. I drove over here to take a look at the house, but there was no sign out front, so I thought I was mistaken. This woman came along with her dog and confirmed that the house was in fact up for sale."

"Okay."

"I walked around to get a closer look, found the back door open and decided to take a peek inside."

"And you just happened to find a head in the sink."

"Well, I wouldn't say 'just happened,' but there was a head in the sink."

They sat on the terrace while a police forensic team in white jump suits filed in and out of the house. A couple of firemen beside the pool sucked on cigarettes. A knot of para-medics lingered beside an ambulance in the drive. He could hear the squawk of police radios from the squad cars lined along the street. Uniformed officers were everywhere. Tree was amazed how quietly everyone worked. The cops didn't make jokes like their television counterparts.

"The last time we met, Tree, you were snooping around looking for Dara Rait."

"That's right."

"Then maybe you came here looking for her."

That caught Tree by surprise. "The woman in there is Dara Rait?"

"I didn't say that. I asked you if you were here looking for Dara."

"No, I wasn't."

"Pretty wild coincidence, don't you think, Tree?" Mel said. "Of all the houses in Fort Myers, you happen to show up at the one with a corpse in it."

"I guess it is, yeah."

"And you don't know anything about how it got here?"

"How would I know?"

Nobody answered. Mel abruptly rose and went inside, pushing past one of the emerging forensic techs.

"Every time I see Detective Scott, I get the impression he wants to hit me."

"I don't think he wants to hit you," Cee Jay said. "I think he'd be happy enough to kick your butt around."

"Any idea why he doesn't like me?"

"He thinks you're an asshole."

"What do you think, Detective Boone?"

"You're shaking, Tree. Are you going to be all right?"

"I'm fine." Maybe all this was getting to him more than he thought.

"You want to know what I think? I think you're lying through your teeth." She indicated the scene unfolding around them. "A murder's been committed here, and you're lying about it. That's serious shit."

"I understand," Tree said.

"You understand? What the hell is that supposed to mean? You understand that you've got to stop bullshitting us, is that what you mean?"

"Look, I don't blame you for being upset with me."

"Upset with you? I'm not upset with you, Tree. This isn't like, we keep you in after school. I'm conducting a murder investigation, and I'm expecting you to cooperate."

"You're right, I'm a little shaken up," Tree said. "Give me some time to get a handle on things."

"You need to tell the truth," Cee Jay said. "That's what's going to help you more than anything."

"I am telling you the truth," Tree said. "The trouble is, you don't believe me."

"Yeah, that's the trouble all right."

Cee Jay sat back and exhaled. "Go on home, Tree. Have dinner with your wife. Tell her what happened this afternoon. I don't know what she thinks of you as a detective but I suspect she's going to think a whole lot less when you tell her about this."

She paused, waiting for his response. When there was none, she looked even more impatient.

"The two of you talk it through, and then give me a call. But don't wait too long. You don't call and I find out you're lying or withholding evidence, I swear to God I will arrest you and throw you in jail."

"So you don't want to tell me who that is in there."

"You're not listening to me. I don't want to tell you because I don't know. Now quit asking me questions and get the hell out of here."

He stood up. His legs felt wobbly. He heard Cee Jay Boone say, "Do you want someone to drive you home?"

"No, I can drive."

And he could. By the time he got behind the wheel of his car, he felt better. He crossed the causeway onto Sanibel Island. His mind began to churn through what he should do next and consider how much trouble he was in. He had not lied to the police so much as omitted certain truths, such as the name of his client and how he came to be at the house in the first place. He had promised to keep his relationship with Elizabeth Traven confidential. He didn't think she was capable of cutting anyone's head off, but what about the people she was dealing with—the criminal class as she called them?

No question that the police would be on him again. Detectives Boone and Scott thought he was an ineffectual amateur prone to fainting at the mere sight of a headless corpse. That might work for him, he decided as he parked the car in the drive. Hopefully, they considered him too dumb to know much of anything. Maybe they were right.

He got out of the car and started for the house. Marcello sat beneath a palm tree. "What did you do with my bike?" he said.

12

Your bike's in the house," Tree said.

"I wanted to make sure you didn't take it on me."

"No, I wouldn't do that."

They stood there looking at each other. Marcello appeared tired and pale, and unless Tree was mistaken, he had lost weight since the last time.

"Are you hungry? Would you like something to eat?"

Marcello nodded.

"Come on, let's go inside."

In the kitchen, Tree busied himself preparing tuna salad. Marcello shrugged out of his backpack and laid it on the chair next to him. He gulped down a glass of water. Tree dumped flaked tuna into a bowl and added mayonnaise and diced green onions before Marcello announced he didn't like tuna.

"Why didn't you tell me that earlier?"

"You didn't tell me what you were doing."

"Okay. So what do you want?"

"I don't know."

"Ham? I've got some sliced ham. How about a ham sandwich?"

Marcello nodded. Tree sighed and made him a ham sandwich. Marcello said he didn't want lettuce on it. Tree removed the lettuce and set the sandwich in front of him. Marcello stared at it for a time, as if he thought it might be poisoned. He decided to throw caution to the winds and wolfed it down.

Tree poured him a glass of milk and Marcello finished it off in impressive gulps. Then he ate another sandwich. And three chocolate chip cookies. After he was finished, he looked less drawn and more alert.

Tree said, "Listen, we have to talk about your mother."

"Have you found her?"

"I've been looking for her," Tree said. "I went to an address at the Bon Air Mobile Park."

Marcello just looked at him.

"A woman named Dara," Tree went on. "Dara Rait."

Tree watched to see if the name got a reaction. It didn't.

"She bought that bike for you."

"No she didn't." Marcello was adamant.

"Who bought it?"

He shrugged. "Reno."

"Reno O'Hara bought you the bike?"

"I don't know. Maybe."

"Are Reno and Dara together? Your mom and dad?"

Marcello paused before he mumbled, "She's not my real mother."

Tree folded his arms and leaned against the counter, watching Marcello. "If she's not your real mother, who is she?"

"She's the woman with my dad," Marcello replied. He spoke slowly, as though not certain of the words.

"Reno's your father?"

Marcello nodded. That would explain why Reno turned up at the office. He was looking for Dara. Or Dara and Marcello.

"Your real mom sent you those letters," Tree said.

Marcello nodded.

"But you don't actually know who she is."

"That's why I paid you money," Marcello said. "So you could find my mom, and everything will be all right again."

"Right now, though, everything isn't all right."

"Everything's bad," Marcello mumbled.

"Tell me what's happening."

"Reno? He's pretty mad at me."

"You're hiding from Reno?"

"And his friends."

"Reno's friends?"

"They're looking for me."

"But you don't want them to find you."

"They scare me so I hide from them."

He collected Marcello's plate and the empty milk glass. "Would you like some more milk?"

Marcello shook his head. Tree put the dishes in the sink. He hated dirty dishes in the sink, but he didn't want to take the time to wash them. Not right now, not when he had Marcello's full attention.

He sat down across from the boy. "Marcello, look at me." The boy reluctantly raised his eyes to meet Tree's.

"This is a lot more serious, okay? Things are happening I'm not equipped to handle. You understand, don't you?"

"No," Marcello said.

"I don't want you to get hurt."

Tree paused, waiting for Marcello's acknowledgement. There was none.

"I know you don't like this, but I think it's time to go to the police."

Marcello's face went flat.

"The police can protect you from these bad men you talk about," Tree went on. "I can't do that."

"They can't do anything," Marcello said.

"Yes, they can," Tree insisted. "They've got the training I don't have. If these guys who are after you show up right now, there's nothing I can do. I don't even own a gun."

"You don't have a gun?" Marcello looked surprised.

"No, I don't."

"Gotta go to the bathroom," Marcello said.

"In the meantime, do you want me to call the police?"

"Let me go to the bathroom first," he said.

"Through that door. Down the hall on your left."

Marcello slid off his chair and went out of the kitchen. Tree debated whether to call Cee Jay Boone but that felt like a betrayal. Wait for the kid to come back and then work it out with him. That was the right way to handle this. Tree went to the refrigerator for a Diet Coke. The telephone rang.

"Is this Mr. Tree Callister?" a voice on the other end asked.

"Yes," Tree said, immediately regretting picking up the phone.

"Mr. Callister, my name is Tommy Dobbs. I'm a reporter for the *Island Reporter*. I want to ask you a few questions."

Tree looked toward the bathroom. "What about?"

"You're the guy who found the body in the house on Barrington, correct?"

"That's right," Tree said. "But I've got nothing to say."

"You're a former reporter, right? Used to work for the *Chicago Sun-Times*?"

"What did you say your name was?"

"Dobbs. Tommy Dobbs. When I was a kid, I used to read your stuff. It was syndicated down here."

Marcello still had not come out of the bathroom.

"Tommy, I don't have time for this right now."

"This is amazing. Big-time reporter moves to Sanibel and becomes a private detective. I mean, how weird is that?"

"What's weird about it?"

"No disrespect intended," Tommy hastily amended. "But it's a great story, and I'd like to talk to you."

Still no sign of Marcello. "Some other time, kid."

"'Kid?' I love it. Real old-time newspaper stuff." As though this guy had unearthed an ancient relic from a long dead civilization. Maybe he had.

"Mr. Callister, please, just tell me what you were doing at that house. I've got to get something up on our website."

"I didn't think the day would ever come when I would say this, but 'no comment,'" Tree said.

"Come on, Mr. Callister. You're talking to a fellow journalist here."

"No, I'm not," Tree said and hung up.

He called down the hall. "Marcello?" No answer. "Marcello." More insistent this time.

Tree went along to the bathroom door. It was locked. "Marcello? Come on. Open up." He pounded on the door.

Finally, Tree smashed his shoulder against the door. It shook but did not budge. He hit it again and still the door held. Now he really was angry, at Marcello, at himself and his inability to get anything even close to right. Why, he couldn't even break down a bathroom door.

He heard an outside door open and turned as Freddie poked her head into the hall. "What are you doing?"

"I'm trying to break down the bathroom door."

"Okay. But why are you doing that?"

"Because I goddamn feel like it," he said.

She came along the corridor and put her hand on his arm. "Bad day?"

He couldn't help but laugh.

———

Freddie led Tree outside to the open bathroom window through which Marcello escaped. She suggested Tree crawl through the window into the bathroom and unlock the door from the inside, thus saving them the cost of replacing a door.

Tree told Freddie about his discovery of the body, the police, the encounter with Marcello. She remained calm but her displeasure was evident. He could hardly blame her.

In the kitchen, Freddie poured herself a glass of wine. Tree noticed Marcello's backpack, still lying on the chair where he left it. He picked it up and opened the flap.

"Should you be doing that?" Freddie asked.

"Doing what?"

"Snooping through other people's property."

"I'm a detective," Tree said. "That's what us detectives do. We snoop through other people's property."

"This being a detective appears to allow you to indulge in all sorts of questionable behavior."

There wasn't much inside; a partially-eaten Mars chocolate bar, a bottle of Evian water, half empty; what looked to be a pretty old version of a Gameboy handheld video game; and a dog-eared paperback copy of *To Kill a Mockingbird*.

Freddie picked up the book. "He has good taste." Blue cards dropped out and fell to the floor.

Tree bent to pick them up. "From his mother."

"His real mother?"

"So he says."

There were four greeting cards altogether—blue, engraved with a tiny white heart. Two of them Marcello had already shown him. Two others Tree hadn't seen before. He laid the first unread card on the kitchen table so they could look at it together. He put on his reading glasses.

Hi, my little love,

I'm sorry to say there have been problems I was not expecting. I'm getting past them but they will delay us being together. Please, don't despair. We will be together, I promise. It's just going to take a little longer than I expected, that's all. I hope you're getting these notes, sweetheart, so that you know I miss you every day, and I love you very much. I will be in touch soon.

Mommy

The second card read:

My love,
I'm on my way.
Mommy

"Except she wasn't on her way," Tree said.

"Or maybe she was," Freddie said.

"What do you mean?"

"That woman you found. Maybe that was Marcello's mother coming for him. Maybe this guy O'Hara killed her before she could get to her son."

Tree stared at the four hand-written greeting cards spread out on the kitchen table.

"I'm worried about the boy," Freddie said.

"So am I," Tree said. "This guy Reno O'Hara is after him. Marcello's scared."

"There is something else at work here," Freddie said.

"What's that?"

"I'm not sure I can put my finger on it," Freddie said. "Maybe it's this new Tree Callister. The Sanibel Sunset Detective."

"You think that's a different guy?"

"I wonder if he is, yeah."

"And if he is?"

"I'm not certain about him. I'm not sure what he's up to. He's involved in things I don't know anything about, dead bodies and danger. I'm not sure about this guy. I'm not even certain I like him."

"Hey, it's still me." He tried to hold her. She pulled away.

"I'm serious. I like my old Tree, the dependable fellow who can't find his reading glasses and might not have taken a lot of chances but didn't find dead bodies or receive threats from nasty people or get the police pissed at him."

"Okay, fair enough," Tree said. "But I've got to be honest."

"I wouldn't want you any other way," Freddie said.

"I kind of like the Sanibel Sunset Detective. Life's suddenly a lot more interesting with him around."

"That's fine," Freddie said. "Just make sure the Sanibel Sunset Detective doesn't get Tree Callister killed."

———

Tree tossed and turned for the better part of an hour, unable to sleep. Beside him, Freddie's chest softly rose and fell. He marveled at her. No matter what happened, she slept soundly. He eased himself out of bed and went into the kitchen. He spent ten minutes locating his glasses, resisting the urge to wake up Freddie and ask her where they were. He found the glasses under a copy of *InStyle* magazine. How the blazes did they get there? The blue greeting cards lay on the table where he had left them. He read all four again. Something was familiar. Something he should recognize.

But what?

13

Late the next morning, Tree came out of the office and started across the parking lot. A young man leaned against the Beetle, squinting into the sun, Ichabod Crane-thin, with short bristling hair and Ray-Ban sunglasses. Acne crawled up his neck and danced across cheekbones the color of putty. A faded white shirt was open at the frayed collar. Tree stared. He might have been meeting himself a long time ago.

"Mr. Callister?"

"Don't tell me. You're Tommy Dobbs."

Tommy Dobbs's mouth dropped open. "How did you know?"

"You should separate your lights from your darks," Tree said.

"What?"

"When you're doing a washing. Separate white clothes from dark. That way you won't end up with white shirts that are grey."

"I'd like to talk, Mr. Callister."

"Show up in a clean white shirt, then we'll talk."

"Like I told you on the phone, I need a quote for my story, and also I want to do a color piece about you."

"I don't want you to do a 'color piece' about me."

"You'd be helping out a fellow reporter, Mr. Callister. I

don't need to tell you what a big story this is. How often do we get a murder here, let alone one involving an island resident who is a former newspaperman turned private eye."

As Tree opened his car door, Tommy was practically on top of him, his face anxious behind the Ray-Bans. "I'll be honest with you, Mr. Callister. My editor wanted to pull me off this and put Myron Merrick on it. Myron's sort of the top dog reporter at the *Island Reporter*. He's totally a jerk. I don't think you'd like him."

"I'm not even sure I like you, Tommy."

"Come on, Mr. Callister. You like me. How can you not like me?"

"So far it's been pretty easy."

"Also, I told my editor we had a personal relationship."

"You should not have told him that."

"Well, we do sort of have a personal relationship."

"Tommy, we don't have any relationship at all. Until a few moments ago, you were a voice on the phone. An irritating voice."

"I'm sorry you feel that way, Mr. Callister." Tommy sounded wounded. "Anyway, my editor's letting me stay on the story, but I gotta come up with something. I'm due to be on Twitter in five minutes."

"On what?"

"Twitter. I've got to tweet our readers. Part of the job."

"Do you ever take off those dark glasses, Tommy?"

"No, sir."

"Because you think it's cool?"

"I've only got one eye."

"You're kidding."

"I'm a little self-conscious about it."

Tree shut the car door and said, "Okay, here's what I'll do. I'll give you a quote."

Tommy looked relieved. "Thanks, Mr. Callister. You're saving my ass here, you really are."

"But hold off on any feature for the time being."

"I will get that story, though, right?" Even with the obscuring Ray-Bans, Tree could see that Tommy's face had taken on a more canny expression. Tree wondered if it wasn't too easy to underestimate Tommy Dobbs. The way you might once have underestimated Tree Callister.

"You want that quote or not?"

Tommy fumbled in his pocket and brought out a metal object the size of a cell phone. He stuck it under Tree's nose. "Okay, Mr. Callister. Fire away."

"What's that?"

"It's an Olympus LS-10 voice recorder."

"You don't take notes?"

"Notes?" Tommy looked confused. "What are you talking about?"

"Notes. Writing things down in a notebook."

"Why would you do that when you've got a voice recorder? That way you don't make a mistake with the quote."

Hard to argue that logic.

"I heard there was a house for sale in McGregor Woods and went around to look at it," Tree said. "When I got there, I found the door open. I stepped inside, and that's when I found the body."

"You're a private eye these days, Mr. Callister." Tommy spoke formally into the voice recorder. "Police are speculating you were at the house on a case. Care to comment?"

"I've said all I'm going to say," Tree said.

"Are you going to investigate the murder you uncovered, Mr. Callister?"

"I didn't uncover anything. I found a body."

"How does it feel, Mr. Callister, a former Chicago news man now involved in a murder here in the Fort Myers area?"

"That's enough, Tommy."

A Blackberry suddenly replaced Tommy's digital recorder, thumbs moving adroitly over the keyboard. "What are you doing?"

"Tweeting my readers," Tommy said. "Sending out your quote. Then I do a short piece for our Internet home page, and after that get it on Facebook. This afternoon, I'll add it to my blog."

"Any chance it will ever appear in a newspaper?"

Tommy finished with his Blackberry and produced a small, black Sony Digital Cyber-shot. He pointed it at Tree. "Quick photo," Tommy said.

Tree barely had time to remove his glasses before there was a sharp click. Tommy adjusted the setting.

"Okay. Now I'm gonna get video for the website, if you don't mind, Mr. Callister."

Tree rolled his eyes. Welcome to the new journalism.

14

The Travens lived in a massive house of interlocking grey stone on Captiva Drive. The house was set behind an iron gate among artfully clustered palms. Grecian columns fronted a sweeping staircase guarded by two stone Great Danes. Gleaming white porches ran the length of two floors.

Tree parked the Beetle outside the wall and came through the gate along the drive. The air filled with the low rattle of cicadas. He could hear the occasional car on Captiva. Otherwise, all was silence. The world here, walled and safe and perfectly arranged, appeared deserted, like so much of Florida. The state was full of people, wasn't it? Sometimes Tree wondered.

He climbed a wide sparkling stairway that might have gone all the way to heaven, but stopped at a landing where there was a bell to ring. Almost immediately—as though he'd been waiting—a small, elegant man opened the door. White hair retreated from a sun-burned face. He wore a shirt without a wrinkle in it, so white it hurt the eyes. He must have bought the gleaming black loafers a moment before he opened the door.

"Yes?"

"I'm looking for Mrs. Traven," Tree said. "Is she around?"

"And you are, sir?" The question came with a Spanish accent.

"Tree Callister. I'm doing some work for Mrs. Traven."

"Yes, Mr. Callister." He seemed to recognize Tree's name. "Come inside. Please."

Tree stepped past him into a foyer the size of a football field. The foyer dropped into an equally vast living area. Glass walls framed the waters of Pine Island Sound in a breathtaking panorama.

The house was separated from the water by a sheen of green lawn, intersected by lush gardens. A bird-like girl in a straw hat with a brim you could land a helicopter on, floated among the flowers. Tree caught a glimpse of a thin pale face, before she bent to snip a white flower from a bougainvillea plant.

"Seven bedrooms, eight bathrooms," a voice announced a moment before Elizabeth Traven trailed into view.

She wore a black halter top and white shorts matched with Manolo Blahnik sandals mounted on four-inch heels. One look at Elizabeth Traven in the morning and you wanted to book your Sanibel-Captiva vacation.

"There's also a multi-level terraced pool, and a spa. I've never been in the pool. I don't like them."

The heels clicked to a stop a few feet away. Those pale eyes seemed to bore right through him. "You can have it for eighteen million dollars."

"Thanks," he said.

She turned and click-clicked away. "Come along Mr. Callister. Did you meet Jorge?" Tree glanced at the small perfect man who was Jorge. He was rewarded with a show of perfect teeth.

"He's rather like the fellow who worked for Richard Nixon. What was his name, Jorge?

Jorge actually bowed slightly before he said, "Manolo Sanchez, madam."

"My husband loves Richard Nixon. They should have gone to jail together. Probably would have ended up lovers. Did I just say that?"

Tree looked at her.

"Anyway, Jorge is Brand's Manolo Sanchez. He has worked for my husband since Brand was a teenager. You marry Brand Traven, you also get his trusted scout, Jorge."

Jorge showed all the emotion of a piece of mahogany.

"Jorge reports back to Brand every week on my various comings and goings. Anything unusual about the spelling of your name Mr. Callister? Two l's is it not? I wouldn't want Jorge to misspell your name when he reports to my husband. We wouldn't want any erroneous information going back to him, would we Jorge?"

Jorge said, "No, madam."

Elizabeth gave Jorge a withering look. "Go away and play."

He bowed slightly before disappearing, not quite in a puff of smoke, but close enough. Elizabeth gritted her teeth and said, "That man."

Tree followed her through a kitchen the size of a barn. Gleaming copper pots dangled from a rack above a trio of La Cornue stoves Freddie would have murdered for.

"Would you like something, Mr. Callister? A drink?"

"Not for me, thanks."

They entered a family room filled with photographs. Brand and Elizabeth on their wedding day occupied a prominent position atop a brass trestle table. She was not wearing white, Tree noticed.

Elizabeth threw herself onto a leather sofa the length of the room. "Sit down, Mr. Callister. I thought we agreed we were to meet at your office next week."

Tree seated himself across from her and tried to keeps his eyes off those legs. He said, "That was before certain events occurred."

"Before you found a headless body on Barrington Court?" She sounded as though finding corpses was not so unusual. "You are all over the news."

Tree nodded. "I thought we'd better have a talk before I went much further."

"I suppose you told the police about our association."

"The police would be here by now if I had," Tree said, pleased with himself for having kept his mouth shut.

"I read they haven't identified the body yet. It wasn't Mickey Crowley?"

"This woman was blond and white. It may have been someone named Dara Rait." Elizabeth looked at him blankly.

"Does that mean you don't know anyone by that name?" Tree said.

"Why should I know anyone by that name?"

"What about Reno O'Hara?"

"What about him?"

"Do you know him?"

"Mickey Crowley, Mr. Callister. No one else interests me."

They were interrupted by the arrival of the girl from the garden, mounted on a motorized wheelchair that moved forward with an electronic hum. Without her garden hat, she looked even smaller and more bird-like, with thin brown hair, blunt cut, oversize imploring eyes, and a hesitant smile. In her hand was the bougainvillea flower from the garden. The wheelchair came to an abrupt halt when she saw Tree. The hesitant smile dropped into confusion.

"Oh, sorry, Auntie Elizabeth, I didn't know you had company."

Auntie Elizabeth allowed a flash of irritation before quickly hiding it behind a welcoming smile. "Don't be silly, Hillary. Come in and meet a business associate, Mr. Tree Callister. Mr. Callister, this is my husband's niece, Hillary Traven."

Hillary motored over to shake Tree's hand. "It's a pleasure to meet you, sir," she said, making it sound as though it genuinely was a pleasure.

She showed him the flower. "Isn't it just the most beautiful thing? Florida flowers are so bright and lovely, don't you think? The bougainvillea was first discovered in Brazil by a French botanist who named it after the explorer and naval admiral, Louis-Antoine de Bougainville. They were traveling together at the time. Did you know that, Mr. Callister?"

"No I didn't," Tree said.

"Hillary is thirteen," Elizabeth said. "A very precocious thirteen."

"Are you visiting?" Tree asked.

"From Wisconsin," she said. "Uncle Brand and Auntie Elizabeth are putting up with me. Well, not Uncle Brand so much, at least not right now."

"I wish you wouldn't call me auntie," Elizabeth said.

Hillary appeared not hear. "What about you, Auntie Elizabeth? Did you know about the bougainvillea? I looked it up on Wikipedia. I'm always looking up things there. Do you, Mr. Callister? Do you use Wikipedia?"

"Hillary, darling," Elizabeth said patiently, "Mr. Callister and I are in the middle of a business conversation."

Hillary's pale face lost its happy sheen. "Oh? Sorry. I shouldn't interrupt. You're not supposed to interrupt are you? Not when you're my age."

"It's all right," Tree said.

She thrust the flower into his hands. "There. A peace offering. Forgive me?"

"No problem," Tree said, uttering a phrase he had taken a blood oath never to use.

Hillary flashed a smile at her auntie. "Are we having lunch?"

"Of course, my dear. Mr. Callister and I are just finishing up. I'll join you in a few minutes."

Hillary turned her wheelchair around and started out of the room. When she was gone, Elizabeth's face darkened. "Brand absolutely adores her. The daughter he never had, I suppose."

"She's charming," Tree said.

"I'm glad you think so." Elizabeth said it in a way that suggested she didn't.

"Where were we, Mr. Callister?"

"Finding dead people."

"Yes, yes, headless corpses who aren't Mickey Crowley. We haven't moved forward very far then, have we?"

"What would you like me to do?"

"Nothing has changed. I still want information about Mickey Crowley."

"All right. But you should know the police are all over me."

"That won't stop a man of your resourcefulness."

Tree couldn't help but smile. A man of his resourcefulness, indeed.

Elizabeth rose in her heels, towering above him. He half expected her to snap a whip. "Good to see you, Mr. Callister."

"Are we still meeting next week?"

"At which time, Mr. Callister, I'm hoping you have a good deal more information than you do right now."

15

Yellow crime scene tape marked the house at Barrington Court. Two vans with "Sanibel Biohazard" printed in big letters inside the chalk outline of a body were parked in the driveway.

Tree parked his Beetle on the street. As he walked toward the house, two figures in bright blue plastic Tyvek suits emerged. They wore goggles and respirators, their feet clad in plastic shoe covers. They carried big green bags that they placed in the back of one of the vans. Tree approached them.

"Is one of you Todd Jackson?"

The smaller of the two talked through his respirator and sounded as though he had arrived from another planet. "Todd's inside."

"I'm a friend of his," Tree said. "Any chance I could have a word with him?"

The guy nodded and disappeared into the house. A couple of moments later, Todd came out through the garage, removing his respirator and goggles. His smooth brown face was drenched in perspiration. He grinned when he saw Tree.

"Hey, Tree, what are you doing? Returning to the scene of the crime?"

The two men shook hands and walked together down the drive to the second van. Todd opened the side door and got a bottle of water out of a cooler. He offered one to Tree, who shook his head.

"What's it like in there?" he asked.

"You found the body, huh? So you got some idea. For us, it's the usual deal. A lot of blood because they hacked off her head. Looks like they used an axe or something.

"An axe?"

"Hatchet. Something like that. A real mess. And of course we had a head in the sink. Not every day you get that. Another big mess. You want to see inside?"

"Can I?"

"Don't see why not. We're in there, so it's been released as a crime scene. Besides, ain't no cops around for the moment. Come on. I'll show you what I do for my daily bread."

Tree wasn't anxious to go back inside the house, but he was supposed to be a detective, and this is what detectives did. They revisited the scene of axe murders.

Scott got him outfitted in a Tyvek suit, shoe covers, goggles, respirator, the whole biohazard package. They stepped inside. This time the air filled not with the stench of death but with the sharp nostril-cleaning tang of ammonium.

"Here's the deal on CTS Decon—that's Crime and Trauma Scene Decontamination to you. Bloodborne pathogens, bodily fluids that are still in floors, carpets, baseboards or walls, all that shit can lead to mould, bacteria, and fungus. People in the house can become sick months or even years later if we don't do our job properly."

A large silver canister-like vacuum stood next to the kitchen counter. They had mostly finished in here. The sink sparkled through the dimness. No human head occupied that gleaming cavity.

In the dining room, workmen used small shovels to lift lumps of congealed blood into plastic containers lined with heavy-duty bags. Others worked on mopping up the dark brown dried blood smeared throughout the room.

"We use enzyme solvent to liquefy the blood so we can get it off the floor, along with urine and other potentially infectious materials or OPIM, as we like to call them."

"An acronym Ray would love," Tree said.

"You can impress him at Fun Friday."

"I doubt anything I do or say is going to impress Ray Dayton."

"You know he's jealous," Todd said.

"Of me? You're not serious."

"He's got a crush on your wife." Tree looked at him. Todd shrugged. "Therefore, he's jealous of you. You can see that, can't you?"

"I'd like to think he hired Freddie for her brains and ability," Tree said.

"He did. But in the meantime, he thinks he's fallen in love with her."

Tree decided it was time to change the subject. He nodded in the direction of the table where he had found the woman's torso. "How long do you think she was dead?"

"The body starts to decompose within fifteen minutes after death," Todd said. "So by the time we got here, I'd say she'd been dead for a couple of days."

"Do the police have any idea who she is?"

"If they know, they're not telling us. Of course, they don't tell us much of anything. I hear you were looking for a short sale when you found the woman—or were you playing detective?"

"I don't know if I would call it playing," Tree said.

Todd laughed. "Don't worry. Your secret's safe with me. The cops probably don't believe you, anyway. So what about it, Tree. You serious about this detective thing?"

"Look at me. I'm standing around watching you guys clean up OPIM."

"Whatever went on in here, it doesn't look as though anyone actually occupied the place. Or else they recently cleaned it out. There's one other thing."

Todd led him to the back of the house into a recreation room. It, too, was empty except for a hospital gurney in the middle of the room.

"What's that doing here?"

"We wondered the same thing. When we got in here, I thought for sure they were using the place as a meth lab. We do a lot of those, let me tell you. But it was clean, nothing like you usually run into when you find a house they're using to make street-grade methamphetamine, really nasty stuff like acetone, methanol, ammonia, benzene, iodine and hydrochloric acid. It all leaves a toxic residue that coats every surface and stays in the air, so there's no doubt about what's gone on."

Tree ran his hand along the gurney. "So what did go on here?"

"We know one thing."

"What's that?"

"They used the place to amputate a woman's head. Someone was a very unhappy camper."

———

Tree got out of his Tyvek suit and the shoe covers and gloves and placed them in a plastic container. Todd said goodbye and went back inside. Tree stood on the drive inhaling fresh Florida air. The elderly woman with the Jack Russell came along the street. She stopped when she saw Tree. The dog yapped a couple of times and bounced around on the sidewalk, delighted to see him. The woman did not seem nearly so pleased.

"Sure, I remember you." She eyed him suspiciously. "The guy looking for the short sale."

"That's right," Tree said. "Tree Callister."

"They mentioned you on the news last night." A black mark against him.

"I don't know your name."

She looked him up and down carefully before she said, "Myrna."

"Well, Myrna, I'm still interested in this house."

She looked surprised. "But they found a dead body—well, I guess it was you, wasn't it? You found a dead body."

"A terrible experience, no doubt about it. But it's still a lovely house, and a good deal is a good deal. But I hear conflicting stories about who owns it. That guy in Orlando you talked about, you sure he's the owner?"

"As far a I know. But then as far as I know usually isn't so far at all. Talk to the real estate people. They can set you straight, I suppose."

"I talked to them. They don't want to say too much about the ownership. I keep hearing the name Michelle Crowley."

"It's like I told you before, never heard that name. Not unless it's the housekeeper."

"There's a housekeeper?"

"Used to be. Saw her come and go a few times. Figured that's who it was. Haven't seen her for a couple of weeks, come to think of it. Why? You interested in a housekeeper?"

"You never know," Tree said. "I wouldn't mind getting in touch with her to see if she'd be interested in staying on if I decide to buy."

"I think she works part time at Jerry's."

"Jerry's Supermarket?"

"In the coffee shop."

"How do you know that?"

"I saw her there," Myrna said.

16

Half of Jerry's was a supermarket, the other half a cheerful coffee shop where the locals congregated for breakfast and gossip. The place had pretty much emptied out by the time Tree got there. Two waitresses chatted against a sideboard at the back of the room. No sign of an African American waitress who might be Michelle Crowley.

Disappointed, he took a table by the window. One of the waitresses broke off her conversation, grabbed a coffee pot off a warmer, and hurried over with a menu.

"I'm Liz," she said. "Your server will be here in a moment."

"You're not my server?" Tree said, taking the menu from her.

"This morning Michelle will be pleased to help you."

Minutes later, Michelle appeared from the back, smoothing her hair, straightening her apron before heading to his table. She fit the description Elizabeth Traven provided for Mickey Crowley, except tinier and cuter. Tree made his reading glasses disappear.

"Hey there, I'm Mickey," she said. "Have you decided on anything?"

"How's your smoked salmon omelet?"

"Look's like you up for a little experimentation first thing in the morning," she said with a grin.

"I've decided to live a little more dangerously."

"Isn't that just how we all live here on Sanibel? A little more dangerously? So go for it, man. Walk on the wild side. Order up that smoked salmon omelet."

Impish humor played in her eyes. There was a wry twist to that full mouth.

"Guess I'd better order it then, otherwise, what are you going to think of me?"

"Seeing as how that's what you're having, nothing but the nicest things." She gave him one more smile before plucking the menu from him and sashaying away.

He reminded himself that this young, sexy woman may have shared a house with a headless corpse. Maybe she helped remove the head. He reminded himself a couple of more times watching her serve other customers. Then she came back with his omelet.

"I forgot to ask you what kind of toast you wanted. But you look like a whole wheat kind of guy, so I brought you whole wheat."

"As it happens, I am a whole wheat kind of guy," he said.

"I can tell that about customers."

"What kind of toast they like?"

"What kind of people they are."

"What kind am I?"

"The flirt kind," she said with another grin. Her eyes flashed again, and she was gone. Was he? The flirt kind? It had been a long time since anyone accused him of that. He bit into his omelet. Don't let her distract you, he told himself. He was a detective, not a flirt. Flirting was part of his clever disguise.

"What did you think?" she asked when he finished.

"The walk on the wild side was worth it," Tree said.

"It always is, man. It always is."

"You think so?"

"Hey, when you're my age, why not? What have you got to lose?"

"What? You think I'm too old for the wild side?"

"Are you kidding? You're the man who ordered the smoked salmon omelet aren't you?"

"I'm the guy."

"Then you don't just walk on the wild side, my friend, you *run*." They both laughed, and then she was all business: "Can I bring you anything else?"

"Just the check."

She pushed the check onto the table. "There you go." She heaved a sigh.

"Long day?" Tree inquired.

"Just that I got one of these—I guess you'd call him demanding. I don't get all the sleep a girl should."

"Too much walking on the wild side?"

"Something like that," she laughed. "Anyway, I'm off at four today, so it's not so bad."

Tree slipped out from the table and got to his feet. "You made it very pleasant," he said. "Thanks."

"Make sure you leave me a million dollar tip," she said.

"Done."

"That's my man."

———

Michelle Crowley had a demanding boyfriend? What about her beloved husband, Dwayne, cooling his heels up at Coleman?

Back at the office, he googled Michelle Crowley's name but that didn't yield anything. She wasn't on Facebook or Linkedin or any of the other social networking sites that he could easily access.

He ran Dwayne Crowley through the inmate locator on the Coleman Prison website. Dwayne was there all right. The inmate locator didn't give much information. Dwayne Robert Crowley was twenty-nine years old and would be released sometime this year.

He had more luck at Prisonlife.com. Dwayne had listed himself on the website's Pen Pals section. His photo showed a pumped, pasty-faced guy—a face fearsome enough to cause widows to faint and orphans to break into tears. What was visible of his right shoulder was adorned with tattoos like black flames.

"This open-minded individual is a Leo who loves to laugh almost as much as enjoying seeing others laugh," he wrote. "I love life as I look at it as a GRAND ADVENTURE."

His message continued: "I enjoy working out, cooking, outdoors, traveling, listening to music, reading and love pets. Since my incarceration, I have brightened my horizons by taking vocational classes and am currently taking a course to be a professional fitness trainer.

"In the last year I have strived to better myself mentally as well as physically, but still feel incomplete and hope to find that special someone to share some time with while I get through these long, lonely days and nights. Could that someone be you?

"I would love to get to know a woman who is also open-minded, understanding and who would love to share a laugh with a kind-hearted guy. I know you are out there in hopes of crossing each other's paths, so I'm sending this SOS in search of that special someone."

Hard to resist a loving soul like Dwayne Crowley. Every woman's dream man. Never mind that he was sitting in a maximum security prison. A minor impediment to true love. Hopefully, a prospective partner would not be put off further by the fact that wonderful Dwayne supposedly was married to loyal Mickey, presumably unaware that her husband was sending out SOS messages to "that special someone," not his wife.

17

A couple of minutes after four o'clock, Mickey Crowley, still in her uniform, came down the ramp from Jerry's and walked to a dusty black pickup. She unlocked the door, got in, and then drove out onto Periwinkle Way. Tree followed her east off the island. Mickey drove along McGregor Boulevard onto Summerlin Trail, and then headed south on Tamiami Trail.

By the time Tamiami Trail became Ninth Street and the well-appointed shops and restaurants of downtown Naples, dusk was falling. Mickey turned left at Tenth Street and went down a block or so before swerving into an apartment complex.

Tree parked his car in time to see Mickey hurry up a flight of stairs in a two-storey block adjacent to the street. Halfway along the walkway, a shaft of yellow light appeared, and Mickey disappeared into it.

Tree went back to his car and got in. From this vantage point, he had a good view of Mickey's apartment. Maybe this was where she lived, and she was home for the night watching *Dancing With the Stars*. Here he was sitting in the dark, feeling like an idiot.

His cell phone rang. He looked at the readout: Freddie.

"What are you doing?"

"I'm on stakeout," he said.

"You're on what?"

"Stakeout. I'm watching someone's apartment."

"Where?"

"In Naples."

"You're watching an apartment in Naples?" Freddie was not doing a great job keeping incredulity out of her voice. "Why are you doing that?"

"It's Mickey Crowley, the woman Elizabeth Traven hired me to look into."

"You found her?"

"Don't sound so surprised."

"What's she doing?"

"Right now? Sitting in an apartment on Tenth Street."

"You should have phoned, Tree. I'm sitting here waiting for you."

"I'm sorry. In all the excitement, I forgot."

"There's excitement in sitting outside someone's apartment?"

"So far, no."

"Do you have any idea what time you'll be home?"

"I'm not sure about that, either."

"Well, don't expect me to be here when you get back."

"What?"

She chuckled. "That's the line in the movies, isn't it? You know, when the wife or girlfriend doesn't want the hero doing whatever it is he's got to do, isn't that the line she always uses?"

"Something like that," Tree allowed.

"I thought I'd try it out since lately you seem to be running your life more and more like a movie."

"I prefer to think of my life as a cheap detective novel."

"Whatever it is, be careful."

Up on the walkway, the yellow light flared again. "Someone's coming. I'll call you later."

"Tree, I mean it. Be careful."

"I will. Don't worry."

He closed his cell phone. Mickey Crowley in a strapless silver mini-dress descended the stairs, the cute waitress transformed into nighttime Florida hottie.

She carried a beaded purse and leaned against a tall man in a creamy suit. It took Tree a moment to realize the tall man was Reno O'Hara.

They reached the sidewalk arm-in-arm, laughing together, and then disappeared around the corner. Tree waited a few moments before following them onto Sixth Avenue.

Tree squeezed through the crowds on Tamiami Trail, keeping Mickey and Reno in sight as they passed the boutiques and sidewalk cafes, afraid Reno might glance around and spot him. But Reno was oblivious to anything but Mickey.

They arrived at an Italian place. Reno shook hands with the maître d' who seated them at an outside table where they could observe the passing crowd. Menus the size of the tablets from the Mount of Olives were presented.

Tree crossed to the other side of the street for a better view. A waiter delivered drinks—beer for Reno, something tall and colorful with a straw for Mickey. They lifted their glasses in a toast. A third guest arrived. Reno smiled broadly and rose to shake the man's hand.

Jorge, major domo to Elizabeth and Brand Traven, sparkled elegantly in the light from the streaming traffic.

———

Tree watched for a while and then walked back to the apartment complex. He stood at the bottom of the stairs leading to the second floor. He could see a light behind the partially-drawn drapes in the apartment Mickey and Reno had vacated.

He climbed to the top of the stairs and started along the walkway. Someone stepped from the shadows, making him jump. A thug-like character in a T-shirt barely containing rippling muscles focused a dead man's stare.

"Good evening." The bright voice of a harmless retiree headed back to his apartment.

The muscle guy didn't say anything. Tree eased past him, certain this was Dwayne Crowley, Mickey's beloved husband, the sensitive Coleman inmate who would love to share a laugh.

He did not strike Tree as someone interested in sharing laughs.

Tree rounded a corner to a second set of stairs and took them back down to the ground floor. He found himself at the rear of the complex. A pool area glowed under amber lights. A patch of grass ended at a roadway running past Naples Bay.

He followed the road around to where he had parked the Beetle. Mickey Crowley leaned against it, her silver dress shimmering under a street light. She held an unlit cigarette in one hand, the beaded purse in the other. He could see the rose tattoo Elizabeth Traven mentioned, a crimson dab on her bare shoulder. She was humming something he didn't recognize.

"You heard Rihanna's new album?"

"No," Tree said

"I am so into that girl. What she's been through? Her father a crack addict, all that. I didn't even want the download, right? Like I went out and bought the CD."

Tree looked around. No sign, so far, of either Reno or Dwayne. Just Mickey, tattooed and sexy in the night.

She held up the cigarette. "I don't suppose you got a light?"

"Sorry."

"Didn't think you would. You don't look like a smoking kind of guy. I can tell about these things. No smoking. No Rihanna."

"What kind of a guy do I look like, Mickey?"

"Like I told you earlier, a flirt." She smiled. "So I guess you got it, huh? That taste. Stronger than coffee, right? Makes you do crazy things, walking around on three legs, thinking, maybe I can get close, get that taste."

He stared at her, not sure what she was getting at.

"On the one hand, I'm flattered, man. Not pissed off or anything, just flattered that you want to be trailing me around.

Thing is, you got the wrong number here. I mean, really. I am no one to mess with."

"No?"

"Here, let me show you something." She opened her purse and pulled out a gun. Its steel surface gleamed under the street light.

"The Beretta Tomcat. I love it. Lightweight. Easily concealed, carries seven rounds in the magazine, and yet it has great stopping power. Never mind the diamonds, man. This is a girl's best friend."

She held the gun casually, as though she had held a lot guns.

"So you see, my flirty friend, although I'm sure you don't mean any harm, all you want to do is get into my pants, but you are definitely sniffing around a girl with a gun, and that's not healthy. Get my drift?"

"I think so," Tree said.

"Tell you what. Why don't you get in your little car, and drive back to Sanibel or wherever you came from? Next time you come into Jerry's, I'll bring you that smoked salmon omelet, the one that got you started on the wild side, and pour you some coffee, and we'll act like none of this happened."

Tree felt hugely embarrassed. She obviously thought he was some sort of stalker. He had an irrational urge to tell her he was really a detective following her for a client. But that was dumb. This way he could get out of there before Reno or Dwayne showed up to make things really complicated.

"Sorry about this," he said.

"Don't be sorry, man. Just be going."

She stepped away from the car. He went around unlocked the door and got inside. He glanced back at Mickey, silvery in the night, the Beretta Tomcat luminous in her hand.

He had waited a lifetime to have that particular image seared on his brain.

18

Freddie reheated the chicken she had prepared earlier and then sat with him in the kitchen while he ate. Women in short dresses pointing guns made him hungry.

"Manolo Blahnik first thing in the morning, that's impressive."

"They were sandals."

"Nevertheless, four-inch heels when you're just wandering around the house and not even expecting company. There's a woman dedicated to heels."

"She was expecting company."

"You?"

"Well, I phoned before I went over there."

"Aren't rich women supposed to seduce private detectives?"

"It's a state law. You hire a private detective you have to sleep with him."

"Make sure she takes off the Manolo Blahniks first."

"I'll try to keep it in mind."

She watched him eat the chicken for a time. "So, did she?"

"Did she what?"

"Try to seduce you?"

"Freddie, I'm sixty years old."

"That doesn't stop anything."

She watched him eat more chicken. "This is very good," he said between mouthfuls.

"You haven't answered my question."

"Are you kidding? I'm the help."

"So was Lady Chatterley's lover."

He told her most of what had happened that evening, deciding not to say anything about the possible appearance of Dwight Crowley or about Mickey in a silver mini-dress brandishing a gun. No use worrying her unnecessarily. He told her instead about Mickey and Reno O'Hara meeting up with Jorge, the Brands' houseman.

"So what happened after Jorge arrived?"

"Not much," Tree said. "They had dinner. Reno talked a lot. Jorge listened and nodded. Then Jorge talked a little bit. Reno listened and nodded."

"And Mickey?"

"She laughed a lot and put her hand on Jorge's knee."

"How did Jorge react to that?"

"He seemed to like it."

"Then what happened?"

"I decided to get out of there."

"That's it?"

"What else would there be?"

"Me, I would have gone back while they were eating, taken another look at that apartment."

Tree swallowed before he said, "I didn't do that."

"You came home."

"To your loving arms."

Freddie rolled her eyes. "Maybe not so loving, my friend. Not when you're visiting seductive women in expensive sandals and then don't call and the chicken gets cold."

"That's the thing about being a detective," he said. "It's beautiful women in expensive shoes, late nights, cold chicken and grumpy wives."

"I'm not grumpy. Just continuing to wonder what you're doing."

Tree got up and took his plate to the sink and rinsed it under the tap. "I'm not certain what I'm seeing—or whether I'm seeing anything. And what does it mean if, in fact, I am seeing something?"

Freddie sipped the last of her wine. "Let's think about this a moment. You've got a boy who wants you to find his mother. Right?"

"Right."

"And you've got a woman, Elizabeth Traven, with a husband in prison worried about another woman named Michelle Crowley whom she has befriended but is now suspicious of."

"A woman dining with a bad guy named Reno O'Hara."

"The two of them meeting up with a fellow who supposedly works for Elizabeth Traven."

"Jorge. The loyal manservant. Maybe not so loyal."

"Throw in the headless body of an unidentified woman."

"Who I find when I'm looking for Mickey."

"So," Freddie went on, "You've got two separate cases and all of a sudden the inhabitants of one case are crossing over into the other, linked by a murder."

"What does it all mean?"

Freddie said, "You're the detective. You figure it out."

"Thanks a lot."

They went out of the kitchen into the bedroom where one thing led to another and they made love, unusual for a weeknight but entirely welcome. Once again he marveled at this incredible woman, reminded himself as he reminded himself each day, how fortunate he was to have her in his life, and how exceedingly happy she made him. He hung suspended in the dark, holding his wife, loving his wife. He drifted off.

Then he was awake again. What was that?

He sat up in bed. A sliver of light from the hall was the only illumination. Freddie stirred beside him. He fumbled on the side table for his reading glasses. Couldn't find them in the darkness. Shit.

"What is it?" she said.

He put his hand out to silence her. She sat up on an elbow,

head cocked. Listening. "Tree, you do this all the time. It's nothing."

He pushed back the covers and rose out of bed. He paused and listened again. The electronic rush of the air conditioning came back to him.

He stepped into the hall, standing naked, manufactured air raising goose bumps on his skin.

Or was it the air?

Something moved in the other room. No doubt this time. Tree stiffened. A man wearing a balaclava stepped into the light. He stopped when he saw Tree.

"What the hell," he said.

Tree dived back into the bedroom, yelling at Freddie to call 911. He caught a glimpse of her coming off the bed as he closed the door, fumbling with the lock. He shouted again as someone hurled against the door. He tried to turn the lock, but the force from the other side knocked him back.

The door blew open. Freddie called out something he couldn't understand. Dark forms descended, outlined against the uncertain light, shrouded in balaclavas. Strong hands roughly pulled him down, pushing his face into the carpet.

"Where's the kid?" A voice in his ear, low and insistent, cutting through his objecting cries.

When he did not immediately answer, someone smashed his head against the floor. Withering pain seared his brain. Stars exploded through the interior blackness.

"The kid," the voice repeated. "Where is he?"

He was lifted off the floor, wrenched around so that he faced Freddie.

A balaclava-covered form held a knife against her throat. The voice said, "See that? Do you see that, asshole? See what's gonna happen to your wife? Now tell me. Where is the kid?"

"He ran away from us, escaped out a window. Haven't seen him since."

The voice again, edged with frustration. "Bastard. Last time. Tell me."

"He's telling you the truth." A tense affirmation from Freddie. "We don't know where he is."

Tree sensed uncertainty among the intruders, a wordless debate over how far to push this.

"I swear to you, we don't know." His voice desperately breaking the silence. "You're holding a knife to my wife's throat. You think I wouldn't tell you?"

His assailant jerked Tree as though he was on the end of a string, as though throwing him around was the easiest thing in the world. Tree understood in that moment how incredibly powerless he was, how lacking in any ability to put a stop to these violently unfolding events.

"Listen to me. Listen, both of you." The intruder's voice in practical register. It's Dwayne, he thought. Has to be Dwayne. He would listen carefully to every single word Dwayne had to say. He would cooperate. Anything Dwayne wanted.

Whatever form the threat was about to take, it was cut off by the high whine of a siren. Growing louder and more intrusive.

"Shit!" The exclamation came from Freddie's captor. A woman's voice?

Tree became aware that he was no longer being held. The knife wielder of indeterminate sex backed away from Freddie.

The siren ceased. There was silence. He tried to sit up. Stars danced on his eyes. Tree blinked a couple of times, the stars reforming into a single light, cutting through the darkness. Someone bent over him. He made out an acne-rimmed face.

"Mr. Callister," a voice said. "It's me, Tommy. Tommy Dobbs."

"Tommy?" was all Tree could manage.

"I was outside. I saw them come in."

"You were outside? What the hell were you doing outside?"

"I saw them come in, Mr. Callister. I saw them invade your home. When I saw that, I ran back to my car. I've got this police siren, see. I set it off, Mr. Callister. I set off the siren and it saved your life."

Tree turned to Freddie. She lay curled into a tight ball, her body shaking.

Behind him, Tommy Dobbs babbled unintelligibly,
drowned out by another siren, this one further away but coming closer.

Freddie reached out to him. Their hands touched. He
pulled himself against her, held her gently until she stopped
trembling.

19

The uniformed officers who responded to the 911 call waited while Freddie and Tree got some clothes on. More police arrived along with a team of paramedics who urged them to go to the hospital for a proper check-up. Both Tree and Freddie declined to do that.

When Detective Mel Scott got there, Freddie had entered into what Tree called her Cool Professional mode. Icy calm, nothing penetrating the steely shield she threw up around her emotions. Tree, on the other hand, was pretty much a wreck. He noticed his hands shaking, as though he had drunk too much the night before. Or was scared shitless.

Mel sat with Freddy and Tree at the kitchen table, making notes from time to time.

"So nothing is missing?" Tree noticed a couple of the uniformed officers remained in the living room. They, too, made notes. Everyone seemed to be writing. Quit writing, he thought. Get out there and find the bad guys.

"Not as far as we can see," said Freddie. She was dressed in jeans and a T-shirt. There was a cut at the base of her neck where the knife blade had nicked her skin. One of the paramedics had swabbed it with an antibacterial wipe.

"Computers, televisions, jewelry?"

"No, nothing." Her voice sounded so strong, much stronger than his probably would right now. He was happy to stay silent and let Freddie do the talking.

"If they didn't take anything, why do you think they broke in?" Mel was looking at Tree when he said this.

"Tell him." Freddie at full strength. Not to be ignored.

"Marcello. They were looking for Marcello."

"This is the kid who hired you for six bucks?"

"Seven. He says men are after him. That's why he's hiding. Now I know what he's talking about."

"But you say you don't know where Marcello is."

"No."

Mel scratched at his chin and made more notes. Tree wondered how often the detective had to get a buzz cut in order to keep his hair so short. To maintain that look, you must be at the barber all the time.

"They were trying to scare us," Freddie said.

Mel stopped scratching. "Scare you?"

"They wanted to scare the shit out of us. Which they succeeded in doing."

"And you didn't get a look at them?"

"As we told the uniformed officers, we got a look at three dudes wearing balaclavas and what appeared to be plastic surgical gloves."

Tree hadn't noticed the surgical gloves. Good for Freddie. But dudes? Is that what you called intruders these days? *Dudes?*

"Other than the balaclavas, any idea what they were wearing?"

Freddie looked at Tree. "What did you think? To me they appeared to be dressed in track outfits, dark blue or black, with hoodies."

This detail, too, had escaped Tree. He saw only the balaclavas. And the knife at his wife's throat.

"What about this kid, Tommy Dobbs? Any idea what he was doing outside?"

Tree shook his head. "Did he see anything?"

"Nothing that was very helpful," Mel said. "He's a little over-excited at the moment. Keeps repeating that he saved your life."

"There's something else," Freddie said.

"What's that?" Mel said.

"One of them was a woman."

"Yeah? What makes you think that?"

"Her voice. At one point, someone said 'shit.' It sounded like a woman's voice."

Mel's cell phone made a buzzing sound inside his coat pocket. He fished it out as he stood up. "Yeah. Hi." He paused and glanced back at Freddie and Tree. "Yeah, that's fine."

He closed the cell phone and came back to the table. "The two of you up for a little ride?"

———

Mel drove a Ford Escort, Tree seated beside him, Freddie in back. No one spoke. The police radio mounted on the dashboard blinked and buzzed. Tree wanted to say something like "What's this all about, detective?" But it sounded cliché, and Mel's demeanor was foreboding enough to encourage silence.

He turned off Sanibel-Captiva Road onto Bowman's Beach Road and pitch blackness. Flares of distant red and white interrupted the black and soon became a parking lot jammed with official-looking vans and vehicles.

K2 crime scene lights mounted on tripods lit the path winding to the beach. They followed a couple of uniformed officers. More crime scene lights on the beach illuminated a surreal knot of spacemen in white jumpsuits.

Cee Jay Boone popped into view, grim-faced. Once again, Tree was struck by the seriousness of purpose here. No laughing at crime scenes.

"Thanks for coming," Cee Jay said.

"What's going on?" Tree asked.

"This way," she said.

The new arrivals drew everyone's attention. The sand beneath the lights was an arctic landscape marked off by yellow police tape and occupied by a body.

The body lay on a crimson bed against the white, spread-eagled on its back, staring into the starry night. The crimson was blood that had flowed from a ragged gash in the corpse's neck. The corpse wore no shoes. A loose shirt seemed too large, rising up to show a pale swell of belly.

A pair of crime scene specialists shone flashlights along the body, trailing ultraviolet blue light across its torso. They wore orange goggles. When the specialists saw Cee Jay they turned off their flashlights and stepped back so that Tree could get a closer look at the corpse. He felt Freddie's hand in his, squeezing tight.

"Do you recognize this person, Tree?" Cee Jay Boone's voice came from somewhere behind him.

Tree nodded. Freddie looked at him, surprise in her voice: "You do?"

"Who would you say it is, Tree?" Cee Jay's voice again, cool and calm.

"I would say it's Reno O'Hara."

"Then you would be right," Cee Jay said.

20

Tree spent some time looking for his glasses before he put on one of the Florida classic rock stations. He couldn't help himself. The last thing he wanted today was news, suspecting he would be part of it.

He bounced around the kitchen in time to Paul Anka singing "Diana." Freddie appeared in beige and grey, announcing she was off to work. Tree turned down the radio. "You haven't seen my reading glasses, have you?"

She held them up. "I found them on the floor in the bedroom."

"Don't go to work," he said.

"What? You're afraid you'll lose your glasses again? Besides, what am I going to do? Sit around watching you dance to Paul Anka?"

He put on his glasses and had a better view of her. "There was a time when you would have been thrilled to see me dancing to Paul Anka."

She raised a dubious eyebrow. "Better I go to work."

They did not get to bed until past two. Tree had drifted off immediately, but then he awoke an hour later. He could sense her beside him in the dark, suspected she too was awake. Neither of them said anything. Tree eventually fell into a restless sleep, only to be awakened with a start in the morning when the alarm went off as usual at six o'clock.

"We're both upset," he said. "We've been attacked and threatened. You're probably pissed at me."

"What would make you think that?"

"I brought this on. It's my fault."

"It's just that I'm not sure I understand what exactly you've brought on. I don't think you do, either."

"That's where you're wrong," he said.

"Am I?"

"Mickey Crowley saw me in Naples. She told Reno. They picked up Mickey's husband, Dwayne, and came here intending to scare us off. Maybe Dwayne didn't like the idea of his wife being with Reno, so after they finished with us, Dwayne drove Reno over to the beach where he killed him."

"You didn't say any of this to the police."

"Not yet."

"Well, it's probably time to stop keeping these things to yourself. Then the police can handle it. That's the way it should be. The best thing either of us can do is get on with it—and hope we don't have too many nightmares."

"Do you think they will? The police, I mean. Handle it?"

"Yes, because that's what they do. Look at the small army that showed up at Bowman's Beach last night."

"Impressive," Tree admitted.

"That's what the cops bring to the party. So tell them what you know, and let them do their job, which would be to find Dwayne and Mickey and put them away." She looked at her watch. "Meanwhile, I'm late for a meeting."

She was all business, pecking his cheek before flying out the door, looking unnervingly bright and focused despite her lack of sleep.

He told himself he would go to work. Ben E. King sang "Stand By Me." Where had he been when he first heard that song? Couldn't remember. He could remember the first 45 rpm record he ever bought—Mitch Miller and the gang singing "The Yellow Rose of Texas." That must have been, what? 1955? What had possessed him to buy that old chestnut? Elvis was out there stirring things up, and he was listening to Mitch Miller? What was wrong with him?

He sat on the terrace in the sunlight, sipping coffee. From inside, Elvis started on "King Creole." Speak of the devil, he thought. When you listened to oldies radio, Elvis was never far from the microphone. The telephone rang. Tree padded across the pool deck as the phone rang a second time. Pushing open the sliding door, he stepped into the kitchen. A startled Marcello stood by the refrigerator. Tree turned down the radio. The phone rang again.

Marcello looked even more miserable than the last time Tree saw him. He nodded at the radio. "What is that?"

"What do you mean?"

"On the radio."

"Elvis Presley?"

Marcello gave him a blank look.

"You don't know Elvis?"

"You listen to that?" Marcello made the notion sound beyond comprehension.

"People used to think he was black," said Tree, as though that might earn him brownie points.

"Only whites would think that. Nobody I know give that bird the time of day never mind mistake him for black."

The phone had stopped ringing.

"I'm hungry." Marcello returned to staring inside the refrigerator.

"What would you like?"

"Don't know," he said.

Tree led him away from the fridge over to the kitchen table. "How about a sandwich? A ham and cheese sandwich?"

Marcello said, "I'm just really hungry."

"Okay, sit down. I'll get you a glass of milk and a piece of bread. That should hold you until I can make a sandwich. Sound good?"

Marcello nodded and sat at the table. Tree poured milk and buttered a slice of whole wheat bread. The boy gulped the milk and wolfed down the bread. Roy Orbison was singing "Love Hurts."

Marcello frowned at the radio. "Can't believe you listen to that."

"One of my many shortcomings. When's the last time you ate anything?"

Marcello shrugged. "You got my backpack?"

"I've got it."

"Where is it? I want it back."

"Is that why you're here?"

Marcello didn't answer. Tree heated tomato soup and made a ham sandwich with tomatoes, lettuce, and mayonnaise. Marcello slurped the soup and stared at the sandwich. Tentatively he peeled back the bread to peer suspiciously at the sandwich's innards. "I thought you were gonna put cheese in it," he said.

"I couldn't find any cheese," Tree said. "Go ahead. Try it."

Marcello studied the sandwich as though it was an improvised explosive device. He picked it up, nibbled at its edge. When it did not explode, he took a bigger bite, then went at the soup, slurping away with a spoon he held like a shovel in his fist.

Tree took out the backpack from a cupboard beneath the counter and put it on a chair beside Marcello. "I want you to listen to me, okay?"

The boy kept suspicious eyes on the backpack.

"I don't want you to do this again, okay? Disappear like that. I don't know where you're hiding, but you're hurting yourself. You're not getting enough to eat, you're not taking care of yourself. I know you're scared, but you don't have to be scared of me. I'm not going to call the police on you, okay?"

When Marcello didn't say anything, Tree spoke firmly: "Marcello. Okay?"

The boy said, "Those men came here."

"You saw them?"

"I told you they were after me. I don't think you believed me."

"I believed you," Tree said carefully. "But I don't understand why they are after you."

Marcello munched on more of the sandwich. "They don't like me."

"Come on, Marcello, stop this." The same impatience he demonstrated with his own kids. Age hadn't improved his parenting skills.

In a calmer voice he said, "This is really serious stuff. These guys broke into my house. They beat me and held a knife to my wife's throat. So there's a lot more to this than 'gee, they don't like me.' Why don't they like you? What did you do? Or what do you think you might have done. Help me out here."

Marcello continued to work on the sandwich. A tear ran down his cheek. "I just want them to leave me alone."

"I know."

"I'm really tired." He did look drained, as if his sustaining energy had finally run out.

"All right. I'm going to put you in the guest room for a while. But no unexpected departures, okay? I'll help you, but you can't keep disappearing on me. Deal?"

Marcello slowly nodded. Tree put him to bed, tucked him in the way he used to do it with his own kids. The boy was asleep instantly. Sleep reworked Marcello from duplicitous street kid into clear-faced innocent. You could build a Christmas story around him. Tree couldn't help but smile.

He left the bedroom, closing the door softly behind him. That's what you did with sleeping children, was it not? You closed the door softly. It had been a long time since Tree had to worry about such things. But yes, *softly*.

————

Freddie groaned when she got home and saw the sleeping Marcello. She looked at him for a time, her face softening. Hard to resist innocence no matter how troublesome.

They sat on the terrace. Freddie sipped at a glass of chardonnay while they discussed what to do next.

"Last night we almost got killed," Freddie pointed out. "It just strikes me that Marcello is way above our pay grade."

"That doesn't change the fact he is in danger and looking to us for help," Tree said.

"I hate to keep repeating myself but that's all the more reason to turn him over to the police."

"He doesn't like the police, maybe for good reason," Tree countered. "Besides, who knows whether they can even protect him."

"They can protect him a darn sight better than we can."

"Can they? Look, these guys were here last night. They threatened us within an inch of our lives, and searched the place. They couldn't find him and we genuinely didn't know where he was."

"Therefore?"

"They've been here, they didn't find him. They know the police are after them. It's unlikely they will come back any time soon. Therefore, the boy is safest right here in this house—as long as he doesn't run away again."

"What's to stop him from doing that?"

"He promised me."

"Well, then, we don't have to worry, do we?"

They were interrupted by Marcello's shuffling, yawning arrival.

Freddie gave him one of her dazzling smiles. "Hey, Marcello."

Marcello smiled shyly back. "I'm hungry."

Freddie, all thoughts of calling the police pushed away, took Marcello's hand and led him into the kitchen. Tree followed.

Marcello wanted a hamburger. Freddie said she didn't have any hamburger. What about a turkey burger? That sounded okay to Marcello, even though he had never actually eaten a turkey burger.

Half an hour later, they were all seated in the dining room eating turkey burgers. Marcello said he liked his burger just fine, but he didn't much care for the tossed salad Freddie created with tomatoes, cucumbers, and green onions.

Freddie said, "Why don't you at least try it, Marcello?"

Echoing words forever repeated by worried parents. Somewhat to Tree's surprise, Marcello responded by dutifully consuming most of the salad on his plate. Impressive. Already, Marcello had listened much more to Freddie than he ever had to Tree.

"Here's what we'd like you to do, Marcello," Freddie said a few minutes later as he polished off a bowl of caramel pecan ice cream. "We'd like you to stay here with us until we can find your mother or get to the bottom of what the trouble is. How does that sound?"

"Sounds okay," Marcello said.

"The thing is, we don't want you to run away. If that happens there isn't much we can do to help. Understand what I'm saying?"

Marcello said he did.

"That means you're going to have to stay put the next while, and that might be difficult, but I'm counting on you."

Marcello finished his ice cream and got up from the table and placed the bowl in the sink.

"Do me a favor," Freddie said. "Wash out your bowl and put it into the dishwasher."

He returned to the sink, retrieved the bowl and ran hot water over it. Then he opened the fold-down door of the dishwasher and placed the bowl on the lower rack.

"I have to go to the bathroom," he said.

Freddie gave him a warm smile. "It's okay, Marcello. We want you to feel at home. You don't have to ask permission every time you go to the bathroom."

Marcello nodded solemnly and went off down the hall.

They chatted about this and that, not wanting to discuss Marcello or what they would do about him, fearing he might overhear.

Ten minutes passed. Freddie rose from the table. "Marcello," she called.

No answer. Tree followed Freddie to the bathroom. The door was locked. She rattled the knob and called "Marcello." Still no answer. She aimed a murderous look at the door. "Marcello? Are you in there? Marcello?"

Silence.

Freddie stepped back then launched a high kick that struck the door just below the knob. A sharp crack and the wood around the lock splintered. Another kick and the door flew open.

The bathroom was empty; the window was open.

"That little bastard," Freddie said.

Tree went into the guest bedroom and came back a moment later. "His backpack's gone. He must have snuck it into the bathroom before he came into the kitchen."

"He really is a duplicitous little bastard," Freddie said.

"It's all right."

"Why is it all right? How can it be all right? The little shit is going to get himself killed, and I'm going to be guilt-ridden for the rest of my life."

"He will be back," Tree said.

"How do you know that?"

"Because I have something Marcello will want."

He led her into the office and showed her where he had locked the blue cards from Marcello's mother in a desk drawer.

"You didn't believe him," Freddie said.

"I believed him. But I thought I'd take out a little insurance. Also, there is something about these cards that keeps bugging me."

"What's that?"

"If I knew it wouldn't keep bugging me."

The telephone rang. Freddie and Tree traded looks. "What fresh hell is this?"

"To quote Dorothy Parker."

"At times like this, you need Dorothy Parker."

Tree picked up the receiver.

"It's Detective Cee Jay Boone."

He half expected her to say that they had just picked up Marcello.

"There have been some new developments."

"What kind of developments?"

"How's tomorrow morning?"

"For what?" Tree said.

"Meet me at police headquarters. Nine o'clock."

21

The next morning, still smarting over Marcello's latest betrayal, Tree drove to his office. A dozen tourists crowded the reception area, poring over maps and asking questions of the three volunteers on duty. Upstairs, there was a voice mail from his oldest son, Christopher.

"Hey dad, Mom called and said she heard something on the news about you. Someone broke into your house? Hope you and Freddie are okay. Let me know. Whatever happened, I hope it isn't associated with this detective thing. Not sure what that's all about. For what it's worth, Mom says you're the last person in the world who should be a detective. Not sure I don't agree with her. Call me. Love you."

Christopher operated an Internet dating service in Chicago in partnership with his second wife, a former *Playboy* model named Kendra. And he worried about his dad being a private detective? What a curious world Tree now existed in; his son ran an Internet dating service; he was a private detective. Each thought the other crazy.

He called back and got Christopher's voice mail. Tree told the voice mail he was okay, that three men had broken in but they hadn't hurt him or Freddie and ran out before they could take anything. He did not comment on his first wife's observation that he was the last person in the world who should be a detective.

After all, she might be right.

At ten minutes to nine, Tree came down the back stairs and into the parking lot. Tommy Dobbs was just getting out of his car.

"I've been trying to get hold of you," Tommy said.

"Tommy, I don't have time for this right now," Tree said.

"Have you seen my story?"

"No."

"It's online."

"I don't read newspapers online," Tree said.

"The police have been giving me a hard time."

"No kidding. I mean what the hell were you doing outside my house at that time of night?"

"An investigative piece." He sounded defensive.

"An investigative piece? On what?"

"You."

"Tommy, I'm not some organized crime figure. You don't have to stake out my house in the middle of the night."

"Okay, maybe I got carried away, but it's lucky for you I did. I saved you and your wife, didn't I?"

"You keep saying that."

"Because it's true."

"I've got to go," Tree said. He opened his car door and got in.

Tommy leaned in the window. The sunlight glinted off the Ray-Bans and made his acne stand out. A kid, Tree thought. Just a big, skinny kid. He was struck again by the notion that he was staring at himself.

"My editor wants a follow-up," Tommy said.

"That's fine," Tree said, "but I want you to quit following me. You need a quote or something, great. Call me. But don't get all weird about this and turn into some sort of stalker."

"I'm not a stalker." He sounded offended by the notion.

"Then quit acting like one."

He left Tommy standing in the parking lot, shoulders slumped. Marcello and Tommy. He was surrounded by lost boys.

Tree drove along Causeway Road onto Periwinkle Way, keeping his eye on the rearview mirror, half expecting Tommy to follow, relieved when he didn't. The last thing he needed right now was an overzealous young reporter, the ghost of himself, trailing him around.

He turned right onto Dunlop Road and parked in the city hall parking lot. If you veer to the right, you end up at the city hall itself. Tree went up the stairs on the left and then took the long walkway to the bright blue door that marked the entrance to the Sanibel Police Department.

Inside, the offices looked as though they had been renovated the day before. No grimy walls or donut-eating cops here. Everyone looked as though they'd had oatmeal for breakfast. Everyone that is except Cee Jay Boone. She looked as though she had eaten nails and was not happy about it. "You're late."

"I got tied up at the office."

She grunted. "Follow me."

A hallway with a linoleum floor you could eat off of led to a small conference room. Detective Mel Scott slumped in a chair at the head of the table, flanked by an Asian male with spiky hair, wearing a dark suit and a blue tie. It was not every day you saw someone in a tie on Sanibel Island. The kid was practically a tourist attraction.

Seated across from the tourist attraction, an African American woman with glossy hair falling in a smooth wave to her shoulders glanced up from her Blackberry. Her business suit featured purple pinstripes, more elegant than the tourist attraction's suit. Tree looked at her, and then looked again, longing to get out his reading glasses to make sure. His vanity wouldn't allow it.

Cee Jay Boone was saying, "Tree, these are FBI agents. They've come over from Miami to have a word with you."

The Asian male shot to his feet pumping Tree's hand. "Shawn Lazenby."

The woman leaned forward to offer a cool firm handshake. "Savannah Trask."

Even without his glasses on, he could see that in her early forties she still had that breathtaking coffee-smooth complexion. He caught a familiar scent as she took her hand away from his.

Mel Scott gave Tree one of his trademark scowls. "Anything wrong?"

"Not at all," Tree said. "I can't tell you how many times I've been called into police headquarters first thing in the morning and introduced to FBI agents without warning."

Cee Jay Boone said, "Why don't you sit down, Tree? Would you like coffee?"

"I'm wondering if I should call my lawyer."

Cee Jay looked over at Savannah Trask. "What do you think, Agent Trask? Has Tree any reason to call a lawyer?"

"No, of course not." Savannah's eyes fixed on Tree. "We want to ask you a few questions, that's all."

"About what?"

"Please, take a seat," Savannah Trask said.

Tree eased himself into the empty chair.

Cee Jay Boone gave Mel Scott a look. He rose from the table. "We'll leave you to it," he said.

Mel followed Cee Jay out the door. It closed behind them, leaving him alone with the two agents.

"You're a local private detective is that right?" This from Agent Shawn Lazenby. He consulted a notebook on the table in front of him.

"That's right," Tree said.

"How long have you been a detective?"

"A month," Tree said.

Shawn glanced up from his notebook. "You said a month?"

"That's right."

"And you're licensed by the state of Florida?"

"Obviously."

Shawn Lazenby's gaze returned to his notebook.

"You met Reno O'Hara when he came to your office. Is that correct?"

Tree nodded.

"According to the local police, he threatened you."

"That's right. He said he was looking for someone. He thought I knew this person."

"Why do you suppose he thought that?" Savannah Trask's voice was neutral.

"I had no idea," Tree said. "I told him I didn't know what he was talking about."

"Has that changed?" A follow-up question from Savannah.

"Has what changed?"

"I mean, do you now know who Reno was looking for?"

"I understand he was looking for his son, Marcello.

"After he visited your office, did you see Reno again?"

"I was following a woman named Michelle Crowley in connection with another matter. She met up with O'Hara in Naples and had dinner with him. I believe O'Hara might have seen me and was one of three intruders who invaded my house later that night."

"Mickey Crowley being one of the others?"

"Maybe her husband, too. Dwayne Crowley. He was in Coleman, but he might be out now."

"You don't know that for a fact." Shawn Lazenby gave him a sharp look.

"I'm pretty certain I saw him in Naples. For just a moment, but I think it was him. Can't you check this out? It shouldn't take long to find out if Dwayne's still in jail."

Neither agent said anything. Savannah Trask cleared her throat. "Let's go back to Marcello. Do you know where he is?"

"No."

A flash of irritation signaled Savannah's dislike of that answer.

"Whoever killed Reno O'Hara will be looking for the boy," she said. "The sooner we find him, the sooner we can protect him."

"Why would the FBI be interested in either O'Hara or Marcello?"

Shawn Lazenby said, "That's information we'd just as soon not divulge at this juncture."

"At this juncture," Tree repeated. "At what juncture might you be prepared to divulge it?"

There was an edge to Savannah's voice. "Are you sure you can't tell us where your client is?"

"No, in fact, I can't. I've tried to reassure him that my wife and I are on his side, that he would be safer with us or with the police. But he's scared. He doesn't trust anyone."

"That's the point, Mr. Callister. We want to help the boy. Running loose the way he is, not only endangers Marcello but you and your wife as well."

"You think I don't know that?"

Savannah Trask rose to her feet, coming into sharper focus, reminding Tree how age can sometimes fail badly when it sets out to defeat beauty.

"If Marcello shows up again, would you let us know?" She handed him a card. "This has my cell phone number."

Her fingers touched his arm. He would like to have said he felt no electrical surge. But he would have been lying.

"We want what's best for the boy, we really do," she said. "Please try to assure him of that if you talk to him. Tell him that he doesn't have anything to fear from us. We can make him safe."

Agent Shawn Lazenby didn't offer a card. Just his hand and a cold smile. "We'll be in touch," he said.

22

A new dynamic was at work in their marriage. Previously, everything revolved around Freddie and her job—Freddie's relocation to Sanibel, Freddie's clashes with Ray Dayton, Freddie arguing for new computer systems, fighting for best practices, wrestling with inventory, staff problems.

All that changed overnight. A job that a week ago was a joke, had, to Tree's amazement, taken center stage. In the evening, Freddie showed scant interest in discussing her day. Instead, she devoured Tree's news, the two of them on the terrace outlined in the gold and crimson of the waning sun, sifting and dissecting what they knew about the case—she called it the case—analyzing the latest intelligence, debating what should be done next.

The case.

He admitted to himself that the case had the effect of making him more duplicitous. It was not that he lied as such; he simply found it easier to withhold certain things. For example, he did not tell Freddie about his interview with the two FBI agents. That is, he did not say anything until he got a telephone call after he'd been home for an hour.

"It's Savannah Trask," said the voice on the other end of the line.

That caused Tree's heart to jolt. It should not have. But it did.

"Are you busy?"

"Well, I'm home." Stupid. Of course he was home.

"Can you get away? I'd like to have a word with you."

"When?"

"Now. I'm at the South Seas Resort. Suite 5-1-9."

The line went dead. He hung up and turned to find Freddie leaning against the kitchen counter, watching him expectantly.

"That was the FBI agent I was just going to tell you about," he said.

"The FBI?" Freddie frowned.

"They interviewed me this morning."

"About what?"

"About Marcello."

"What did you tell them?"

"I was honest with them," he said trying to head off any discussion around the degree of his honesty. "The good news is they want to find Marcello as badly as we do, and protect him."

"Protect him from what exactly?"

"They don't mind me telling them things, but they don't say much back. Anyway, that was one of the agents. They want to talk to me again."

"Tonight?"

"They're staying at the South Seas."

"Do you want me to go with you?"

He hesitated. "I'd better do this alone."

"Are you sure?"

Not really, he thought. He really wasn't sure of anything, least of all how he was going to handle this.

———

Driving to the South Seas Resort, Tree imagined Savannah Trask answering the door in lingerie. Exactly what kind of lingerie he couldn't decide. Possibly something in line with the Gold Medal paperback novels he devoured as a teenager. Their covers invariably featured beautiful women spilling out of scanty underwear. The thought left him unexpectedly short of breath and feeling a little guilty. Did he want to be seduced? Ridiculous. He was going over there to get the meeting over with and get back home.

Tree turned through the South Seas entrance gate and parked in the lot. Savannah opened her door as soon as he knocked. No lingerie. He felt curiously and ridiculously relieved. Savannah wore sensible shorts and an oversize T-shirt with FBI in big letters—in case Tree forgot who she was, and the potential danger she represented.

"Come in," she said in that clipped, professional manner of hers.

A large travel bag lay open on a king-size bed. Business clothes hung neatly in the louvered closets. An Apple notebook was set up on the desk. The new Michael Lewis book was on a night table beside the bed, right next to her copy of *The Economist*. Savannah Trask looked as though she was planning to stay a while.

"Can I call to get you something?"

"No, I'm fine, thanks."

"Why don't we sit at the table over there?"

A delicate white table on dainty legs was flanked by two wrought-iron chairs. He sat across from her, settling back, trying to get comfortable and failing.

She smiled. "So what did you think when you saw me this morning?"

He tried a casual smile back but couldn't quite make his mouth work. What did he think? "I'm not quite sure," he said truthfully. "Surprised, I suppose."

To say the least.

"Meeting my ex-boyfriend after all these years, I must say I didn't know what to expect."

"Is that what I am?"

"The white bread Chicago newspaperman and the naïve young African American law student. That was us, wasn't it?"

"So now the law student is an FBI agent," he said.

"That surprises you?"

"I thought you'd end up as a partner in a high-powered law firm in either Chicago or New York."

"Well, you can imagine my shock to discover my old roommate, the veteran newspaperman, is out of the business entirely, and married yet again—although I suppose I shouldn't be surprised about the married part. You always did like being married, Tree."

"Or maybe I didn't like it at all," he said. "Why I kept failing at it."

"Are you failing this time? What number is this? Four? Five?"

"Four," he said. "And the answer is no, not this time."

"Good for you. So here you are on Sanibel Island, a private detective of all things."

She paused to give him a chance to respond. When he didn't she leaned forward, those grey eyes bright with—what?—inquisitiveness? Challenge?

"I mean, come on Tree, are you really serious about this detective stuff?"

"Savannah, let's get to the point of why I'm here, okay? My wife's waiting for me at home."

She sat back in her chair, darkness descending. If past history was any indication, the time for trying to manipulate the situation was over. Time to administer the blunt instrument.

"All right, the point is two murders have been committed. The Sanibel Island police do not rule you out as a possible suspect in both cases. Are you aware of that?"

He tried not to look shocked. "No, I wasn't aware of that."

"They don't believe you're telling them everything you know about either case. What's more, they believe you are keeping the whereabouts of the boy from them."

"What do you think, Savannah?"

She leaned forward, face intense. "Do I think you're being completely honest? No, I don't."

He did not recall honesty being one of Savannah's strong points, either.

"How can I be honest with you?"

"Tell me where Marcello is."

"I told you before, I don't know. I said it to the police. I said it to the people who broke into my house the other night. No one seems to believe me, but I keep saying the same thing over and over again."

"Maybe because everyone has a hard time imagining that a twelve-year-old boy can stay hidden without some adult help."

"Why is the FBI so interested in him?"

"He's an important part of an ongoing investigation."

"And you're investigating what, exactly?"

"I'm part of a probe into the activities of a man named Brand Traven."

Now that really did surprise him.

"You think Marcello and these murders are somehow connected to Brand Traven?"

"That's what Agent Lazenby and myself are here to find out."

"What about the woman I found on Barrington Court?"

"What about her?"

"Has she been identified? If I'm out there knocking people off, I'd at least like to know who they are."

She hesitated before she said, "The woman's name is Dara Rait. But I believe you already know that."

"I know what I told the police, that she bought a bike for Marcello."

"Supposedly, she's an artist. Runs a little shop in Fort Myers Beach. But that's probably a front."

"A front for what?"

"Dara was a former sex trade worker who supplied young women from South America and Mexico to various escort services along the West Coast. We think that's how she became involved with Reno O'Hara."

"Who stands a lot better chance of being Dara's killer than I do."

"As we say, the investigation is still ongoing."

"What was she doing at that house?"

"Dara rented the place about a month ago. We're not sure why. Maybe to house the women she brought up from the South. She never lived there."

"Only died."

"That's right," Savannah said.

"Like I said, Dara bought a bike for Marcello," Tree said. "I tracked her to an address at the Bon Air Mobile Park in Fort Myers Beach. I thought she might be Marcello's mother."

"But she isn't."

"Marcello says she isn't."

"The police think they were using the Bon Air to house women. How did you end up at the house on Barrington? And don't tell me you thought it was up for sale."

"I was looking for Mickey Crowley."

"A call girl from Naples."

"I thought she was a waitress."

"Briefly. She's quit her job and disappeared. Who wants to know the whereabouts of Mickey Crowley?"

"My client wishes to remain anonymous."

"Your client does, huh? You know, Tree, I've ended up telling you a quite a bit this evening. You haven't told me much of anything."

She got to her feet. The FBI letters on her T-shirt looked ten-feet tall. "Think over what we've talked about," she said in that tight, clipped voice she probably used arresting drug lords. "Give me a call if you think of anything or Marcello shows up."

"Fair enough," he said.

He stood. She reached out her hand to him. "Good to see you, Tree."

For one wild moment, he thought they would kiss. The moment passed. He shook her hand.

He went to the door and opened it. She called after him. "Tree."

He turned.

"Did you tell your wife?"

He looked back at her.

"About us. Did you tell your wife about the two of us?"

"What about you, Savannah? Did you ever marry?"

"I never made that mistake, Tree. You were a good role model for me."

Cheshire cat grin. Savannah had the moment.

As she always did.

23

She was the only woman who ever wrote him a love letter. Handwritten, composed after a spat. He couldn't remember the details of the fight. But he always remembered the letter. Four wives and none of them ever wrote him a love letter, not even Freddie. But Savannah had. What had he done with it, anyway? Must be around some place.

There was only one problem with the love letter.

Its author did not love him.

They had met on a local current affairs television show. Student lawyers confronting seasoned law enforcement officers and journalists about what they did and how they did it.

Savannah was bright, intelligent, charming, extremely attractive. He was between marriages, but good grief, he told himself, she was twenty years younger. He made himself forget any stupid ideas about getting involved with her. Not that she'd be interested in a million years.

A couple of weeks later, she called. She had some follow-up questions in connection with a project she was doing for one of her courses. Could they get together for a drink?

He could and they did. How had they ended up living together? Crazy. She was too young and just beginning. He was too old and even then suspecting that journalism, in one way or another, was coming to an end.

She had broken up with her boyfriend, a crazed character who threatened her life and might have been a local hoodlum. Or maybe not, depending on her mood. The point was, she needed a place to stay. That's all it was, right? He wasn't going to sleep with her. And then he couldn't keep his hands off her. Or maybe they couldn't keep their hands off each other.

He deluded himself into thinking they were a couple— until he found out she was seeing a local news anchor. Rex tipped him off. He didn't want to see Tree hurt. He had met Savannah, thought her deceitful and manipulative, not a woman to trust. Rex pointed out that the anchor guy had perfect hair. Tree couldn't compete with perfect hair—Rex's conclusion. He was probably right.

Tree thought he knew what was in store dating someone so much younger, but he wasn't prepared for the emotional toll. He didn't care, but he did. One final encounter: the two of them tearing at each other extracting some kind of sexual revenge. He never saw her again after that. She was gone without a trace. He didn't even have a photograph. It was as though she never existed.

Except she did.

Tree had long since gotten over her. Hadn't he? Maybe it was the damned love letter. What was in it, anyway? He would have to find it and reread its contents. No, he wouldn't. He wouldn't have to do anything like that. He reminded himself again: she had not loved him; she still did not love him.

Instead of worrying about an old flame seducing him—a notion that now seemed particularly ludicrous—he should concern himself with a threatening federal agent who strongly suggested he was a prime suspect in two murder cases.

"Hey!"

He turned to see Agent Shawn Lazenby walking-running toward him, fists clenched. He came to a threatening stop inches away from Tree. He was in shirtsleeves, his spiky hair disheveled, face drawn and tense.

"What's up?" he demanded. His eyes spun in their sockets.

"Just getting into my car," Tree managed to say. "Going home."

"What do you think you're doing?"

"What do you mean?" Tree said. "What are you talking about?"

In response, Shawn slammed him back against the Beetle. "Don't screw with me. Okay? *Okay?*"

Part of Tree's brain insisted this had to be a joke. Yet the force of Shawn's presence, the overpowering physical sense of him, screamed it wasn't.

"What's wrong?" Tree tried to keep his voice calm, reasonable.

"What's *wrong?*" The notion of right and wrong appeared to further agitate Shawn. "I tell you what's *wrong*, as opposed to what's *right*. You and Savannah, that's what's *wrong*. That's what's so goddamn *wrong!*"

"I wasn't—"

"I know about you, okay? I know where you're coming from, okay? You can't fool me, mister. You can't do it. So don't even try."

"I'm not trying to do anything," Tree said.

The agent gave him another hard shove. "Don't let me catch you around her again, man. I mean it. Otherwise, it's a sea of trouble. I'm not fooling. Okay? A sea of trouble."

He turned, and as suddenly as he had arrived, Shawn departed, streaking across the parking lot, leaving Tree slumped against his car.

———

Driving back along Captiva Road, he began to calm down, get his mind off Shawn Lazenby's intimidation—what was that all about? A lovesick cop?— and his unsatisfactory performance with Savannah; intimidation of another kind. He focused instead on what he had learned: Reno O'Hara was part of an ongoing FBI investigation into the affairs of Brand Traven.

Savannah had refused to say how Reno was involved with Traven but the pivotal figure appeared to be twelve-year-old Marcello. The police, the intruders at his house and now the FBI, everyone wanted Marcello. What's more, everyone thought Tree knew where he was. Thus everyone threatened him. He should have been scared, he supposed. Instead, he was rather pleased at being invested with a craftiness and deceit that he doubted he possessed. He had no more idea where Marcello was than anyone else.

His cell phone rang. He slowed to fish it out of his pocket, thinking it was Freddie. However, it wasn't Freddie.

"I need to see you, Mr. Callister," Elizabeth Traven said.

24

An American eagle, said to be a replica of the one in the Oval Office, glared down at Tree from atop the sitting room fireplace inside the Sanctuary Golf Club, as though it feared Tree might desire to become a member and therefore must be torn apart.

Elizabeth Traven, crisp and efficient in a canary-yellow summer dress, was seated in the dining room by one of the picture windows. She did not look any happier to see Tree than the eagle as he seated himself across from her.

"Every time I look at a newspaper, Mr. Callister, there you are on the front page."

"Someone broke into my house," he said.

"So I understand. Are you and your wife all right?"

"A little shaken up, that's all."

"Any idea who was responsible?"

"Let's say I have my suspicions." He decided not to say that he thought one of those responsible was Mickey Crowley. He would save that for later.

Elizabeth looked distracted. "This club is part of the Ding Darling Wildlife Refuge. You probably don't know that special water is required to irrigate the greens."

"I didn't know that," Tree said.

"You play golf, Mr. Callister?"

"I don't play anything."

"No favorite sport?"

"If I didn't know better, I might suspect you're trying to change the subject," Tree said.

"Do you think so?" Elizabeth said.

"The FBI has been questioning me."

That triggered the surprise he had been looking for. "What about?"

"They seem to think your husband might be connected to all this."

"All what, Mr. Callister?"

"Mickey Crowley. Her husband Dwayne. A man named Reno O'Hara, his son Marcello."

A smiling boy of a waiter arrived and made a production of unfurling a white linen napkin for Tree. He asked the waiter for a Diet Coke. Elizabeth Traven arched her eyebrows.

"I thought detectives liked a drink," she said.

"I'm the new breed," he said.

The waiter returned with Tree's Diet Coke and menus. The special was grouper. "Life in Florida," Elizabeth said with a sigh. "The sun shines bright, the private detectives arrive with surprises, and the catch of the day is always grouper."

She sent the waiter for another drink before addressing Tree. "So. Let's have it. Did you tell them anything about me?"

"No, I didn't, although perhaps I should have."

"Why should you?"

"Because I could get into a lot of trouble withholding information from federal agents."

He told her about following Michelle Crowley to Naples, her rendezvous with Reno O'Hara, and their cozy dinner with Jorge. When he finished, those opaque, fathomless eyes appraised him coolly. "You've been busy," she said.

"You don't seem at all dismayed that your butler was having dinner with the woman you're supposed to be so worried about."

"I got past dismay a long time ago."

The waiter came back with a second martini. He could hardly keep his eyes off Elizabeth. She appeared oblivious. A rich woman on a budget, she ordered the house salad.

He asked the waiter for a recommendation. "You can't go wrong with the grouper sandwich."

Tree ordered the grouper. The waiter scurried away casting a last, longing glance at Elizabeth.

"I spoke to my husband at some length last night," she said.

"Yes?"

"We both agreed that for whatever reason, you're attracting too much attention."

"I'm attracting too much attention?"

"This situation with the FBI merely confirms what I've suspected, that you're simply too high profile for us, Mr. Callister."

Tree looked at her, dumbfounded.

"We've decided to terminate your employment."

Tree probably should have said something, but for the life of him, he couldn't think of what it might be.

The grouper sandwich arrived, arranged around a foothill of coleslaw. The waiter had eyes only for Elizabeth as he presented her salad. Somewhat wistfully he asked if he could bring anything else. She couldn't be bothered answering. The waiter looked crestfallen. A heartbreaker, Elizabeth Traven.

In more ways than one.

25

I shouldn't be telling you this." Todd Jackson lowered his voice to suggest that was exactly what he was about to do.

The sounds of Friday night football blasted through the Lighthouse, lost from time to time over Mr. Ray's howls of derision. Life on the big screen TV was not unfolding the way it should for the Ray Man.

Tree leaned closer to Todd. "Tell me what?"

"Crazy as it sounds, the police have got you down for that body they found on Bowman's Beach the other night."

"Reno O'Hara?"

"That's the guy. The thinking is you whacked him, and left him on the beach. That's why his pals broke into your place. They were looking for revenge."

"Boy, that's a stretch."

"You think so? Try this one on. They also got their doubts about the corpse on Barrington Court."

Mr. Ray exploded at the TV screen. A helmeted gladiator had offended his sensibilities. Why, he shouted, couldn't the damned referees see what he saw? Were they blind?

Tree raised his voice in order to be heard over Mr. Ray. "What? They seriously think I'm driving around Fort Myers beheading women?"

"Put it this way, they're not ruling it out." Todd sipped his beer.

Someone jostled against Tree. The bar was packed tonight. Freddie was out there somewhere in that sea of beer-drinking humanity. He felt depressed and agitated. Todd was not helping his mood.

"What about it, Tree?"

"You mean did I kill them? Absolutely. Killed them both."

"Jeez, don't tell me that. I could be called to testify."

"Come on, Todd. Get serious."

Todd looked very serious. "I'm only telling you what the police are saying. Trying to be a friend here."

"Even though I could be a double murderer?"

"Who knows what anyone is capable of. I mean the things I see every week? You don't rule out anything. Still, I do have my doubts about you as a killer."

"I appreciate that, Todd."

Mr. Ray elbowed his way through the crowd and pushed himself between Tree and Todd, face flushed. Someone started singing "Blue Spanish Eyes." Mr. Ray shouted over the music.

"Hey, Tree. What's this I hear about you and dead bodies?"

"How are you doing, Ray?"

"You found a body, I hear."

"Detective Tree Callister on the job," Todd said, trying to lighten the moment.

"That's something isn't it? Finding a dead body?" Mr. Ray focused intently on Tree. "Gonna buy you a beer."

"No thanks, Ray."

He looked around. No sign of Freddie.

"What do you mean? I'm offering to buy you a beer."

"I don't drink beer, Ray."

Ray's face had gone slack. "What? I can't buy you a beer, is that it?"

"No, Ray." Todd looked nervous. Tree started away. Ray put his hand on his arm.

"What's the matter with you? What the hell's the matter?"

"Let go of me."

"Ray, take it easy," Todd said. He looked more nervous.

"Take it easy? You expect me to take it easy when I offer to buy a man a beer and he turns me down? He insults me? And you want me to take it easy?"

Ray's voice had risen to alarming levels.

"Ray, take your hands off me," Tree said.

"Take my hands off you? Who the hell do you think you're talking to? I'm a decorated war veteran. You're a loser. You're lucky I give you the time of day."

Tree thought of Savannah Trask threatening him. He thought of Shawn Lazenby shoving him around in a parking lot. Elizabeth Traven firing him. Now this. Enough.

He slugged Ray Dayton.

A stinging pain shot through his fist when it connected with Ray's jaw. Ray's mouth twisted weirdly. His eyes bulged in surprise as he tumbled backward, his glass taking flight. The next thing Todd was holding him, as though Tree might tear Ray apart with his bare hands.

Freddie was beside him. Even with her mouth open, her eyes wide and unblinking, Tree thought she looked irresistible.

———

"I'm not going to lose my job," Freddie said on the way home.

"I punched out your boss," Tree said. He sat beside Freddie in the passenger seat. He felt terrible.

"How's your hand?"

"It hurts."

"You shouldn't hit people with it."

"I don't know what I was thinking," Tree said.

"You weren't thinking, but never mind. I wonder if we should go over to emergency and have them take a look at it."

"On a Friday night? It'll be a zoo. It's fine. I might have sprained it, that's all."

"You could have broken it."

"You don't think I can punch a guy without breaking my hand?"

"I don't know. How many guys have you punched in your life?"

"Dozens," Tree said.

"I hate to say, 'Ray had it coming.' But Ray was cruising for a bruising, as we used to say. What got into you, anyway?"

"Maybe I'm just tired of everyone pushing me around."

"Poor boy, is everyone pushing you around?"

Tree played his trump card.

"Also, I got fired at lunch."

"You saw Marcello? He wants his six bucks back?"

"It was seven, and it wasn't Marcello. Elizabeth Traven."

Freddie was silent for a time. "That's a surprise. Isn't it?"

"I'm attracting too much attention, apparently."

"Now there's a criticism of you I haven't heard before."

"That's what she told me."

They drove in silence until they reached Andy Rosse Lane and Freddie turned into the drive. She stopped the car and looked over at Tree. "Think about why Elizabeth would fire you."

"Right now we've got bigger problems than Elizabeth Traven. Suppose Ray fires you over this."

"You never know."

"You're being very calm, Freddie. What will we do?"

"Live on your detective salary."

"In a cardboard box under an overpass."

"Well, at least we'll be together."

He kissed her and said, "How did you get to be so wonderful?"

"Years of practice. But let's go back to Elizabeth and why she got rid of you."

"I just told you. I'm too high profile."

"Let's say it was something else. For the sake of argument."

"You see? You just can't imagine me getting too much attention."

"Let's say Elizabeth was looking for something and found it."

"What would she be looking for ?"

"What's everyone looking for?"

"Marcello?"

"It would explain why he hasn't come back for those letters."

"So what you're saying is Elizabeth didn't hire me to protect her from Mickey. She hired me because she thought I knew where Marcello was."

"Now is that brilliant detective work or what?" Freddie grinned.

"But why would she want him?"

"I don't know, but she seems to be mixed up with all sorts of people who do."

———

Inside, Freddie yawned, said she was dead tired, kissed him, and went off to bed. He thought more about Marcello. Where did he go each time he disappeared? He knew bad people were looking for him, yet he felt confident enough to leave. That meant he had found a safe place to hide. But where would a twelve-year-old find that place—close enough to get back to Tree and Freddie whenever the spirit moved him?

No. It couldn't be.

His glasses had disappeared. It took him fifteen minutes to finally locate them on top of the microwave. How the hell did they get there? He went out to the garage and turned on the overhead light. Metal filing cabinets from his newspaper days stood in a corner, otherwise the interior was pretty much empty. He stared up at the trap door in the ceiling; the dangling pull-cord.

He yanked at the cord. The accordion staircase folded neatly down. Tree climbed the stairs into the attic above the garage. It had been a long time since he had been up here. The light was dim but he could make out cathedral-like joists supporting the peaked roof, the paint cans he had piled in a corner and then forgotten about, not far from the sleeping bag on the plywood floor. The sleeping bag didn't belong to him. Tree got on his knees, brushing against the Tampa Rays baseball cap. The sleeping bag was a Coleman with goose down insulation. Fairly expensive. The flap dropped open. Someone had stitched a patch into the fabric. The patch was neatly lettered:

Marcello O'Hara
1188 Estero Blvd.
Fort Myers Beach, Fl.
90250

Tree looked at his watch. It was just after ten o'clock.

26

The Fort Myers Beach fishing pier glowed through the darkness. A late-night couple ambled hand-in-hand across Times Square headed for the beach. The vacancy sign flashed on at the Pierview Hotel. The souvenir shops along Estero Boulevard were closed tight. A few college kids shuffled in and out of Nemo's, while the skinny guy behind the counter at Shep's Subs and Tropical Treats eyed his watch. The wood-carved Indian warrior in front of the Cigar Hut didn't give Tree so much as a second glance.

Eleven-eighty-eight Estero Blvd. was a two-story frame shack painted ocean blue. A multi-colored sign over the door said "Dara." Painted street scenes and ocean views with palm trees were framed and mounted in the window. The interior was dark.

Tree stepped back and looked at the second floor. A light burned in an upper window, illuminating the staircase running up the side of the building. He was standing there, debating what to do next, when the door at the top of the stairs opened, and a woman stepped out.

Mickey Crowley in jeans and a tank top, not as flashy at Fort Myers Beach as she had been in Naples, came down the stairs, turned, and called back.

A man appeared on the landing. He cradled a limp bundle in his arms. The bundle was a little boy.

Marcello.

The man came down the stairs. Tree couldn't quite make him out.

The man followed Mickey to a black SUV parked behind a lattice wall. Tree could see Mickey slide behind the wheel. The man opened the rear door and pushed Marcello inside. He closed the door, waved at Mickey, and then turned to go out onto the street. That's when Tree got a pretty good look at him.

He couldn't say for certain it was Detective Mel Scott, but it sure looked a lot like him.

———

Mickey drove over the causeway onto San Carlos Boulevard. When she turned left onto Summerlin Road, Tree began to suspect where she was headed.

Traffic was light at this time of night so Tree had no trouble keeping the SUV's taillights in view. His cell phone buzzed and jumped on the passenger seat. Freddie. She had probably awakened and found him missing. He decided not to answer it. He had enough to contend with right now.

As soon as the SUV came off onto Periwinkle Way, the traffic abruptly dwindled. Reflexively, Tree fell further back, fearing Mickey would realize she was being followed.

But apparently Mickey had no such concerns as she came along Sanibel-Captiva Road. It didn't take her long to reach the Traven house.

The front drive was bathed in sodium light like a stairway to heaven. Only a Busby Berkeley chorus line singing "We're In the Money" was missing.

Tree waited until Mickey's SUV drove through the electric gates, and then he pulled the Beetle over to the shoulder south of the entrance. He sat for a time, summoning the nerve to do what he was about to do.

He must be out of his mind.

He thought about phoning Freddie. But she would merely confirm what he was thinking, that in fact he was out of his mind and should immediately come home.

He got out of the car, closed the door, and strode through the gate, up the lighted drive, feeling terribly exposed, thinking someone would jump him.

No one did.

Tree climbed the staircase, crossed the porch and tried the door. To his surprise, it opened. He stepped inside the foyer, footsteps echoing against Carrara marble tiles. He expected Jorge to appear, demanding to know what he was doing in the house at this time of night. But there was no Jorge. He heard distant music.

Tree went along a sisal-carpeted hall. Voices came toward him. There was a door to the right. He opened it and found himself in a dimly-lit bedroom.

The voices grew nearer. "It's up to you, of course, but I don't see the problem."

A second voice said, "The problem is them, my friend, the problem is them."

"Always a challenge. A certain type of person agrees to this, and they are usually not easy to deal with."

"These are worse," the second voice said. "At least she is."

Two men passed, heads bent together. One man wore a green hospital smock.

"Anyway," said the first voice, "it's finished tonight."

"Can't be too soon for me."

The voices trailed off. Tree waited a minute or so before stepping back into the hall. He reached the door at the end, hesitated a moment, and then threw it open.

A flat screen television dominated a small room. Tree had never seen such a big TV, would not have known they even made them that size. Nicole Kidman in high definition loomed above Marcello on a chaise lounge. Tree thought the boy asleep, but as he bent down he could see he was awake, staring listlessly at the screen.

"Marcello."

The boy looked at him with bleary, drugged eyes. A watery smile didn't quite work.

"You all right?" Tree said.

The boy slowly turned his head back and forth. "They want to—"

"What is it, Marcello?" Tree said.

"Operation." In a voice so slurry, Tree wasn't certain he had heard him correctly.

"Operation? Is that what you're saying?"

The boy nodded. "Don't want operation. Don't want it."

"I'm going to get you out of here, okay?"

"No operation."

"No," Tree said.

He gathered Marcello in his arms and carried him out into the hall, back through the house and outside into the glare of the sodium lights. Marcello opened his eyes, moved his lips, but said nothing. Tree took a deep breath and started down the steps.

He came out the gate and got to his car, dropping Marcello into the passenger seat, wrapping a seat belt around him. Then Tree crawled in the driver's side and started the engine.

What had he done? he asked himself as he sped away along Captiva Drive.

What the hell had he done?

27

I can't believe you did it," Freddie said when he arrived home with Marcello and told her what happened.

"I can't believe you just walked into someone's house, picked up a little boy and carried him out again," Freddie continued. "What's more—and this is the part I really have trouble with—I can't believe you did it alone. I can't believe you left me lying here, went out in the middle of the night, and did this."

"If I woke you up and told you what I was going to do, you would have stopped me."

"I would have gone with you," she said.

"Besides, I wasn't so sure what I was going to do until I did it. Frankly, I'm almost as surprised at myself as you are."

"We should call the police," Freddie said.

"No, we shouldn't," Tree said. He then told her about seeing Mel Scott on Estero Boulevard.

"Are you certain it was him?"

"Certain enough that it makes sense why Marcello doesn't want to have anything to do with the police. As far as he's concerned, the police are in cahoots with the people who want to hurt him."

"Including Elizabeth Traven."

"Including Elizabeth Traven," he said.

"What a mess," she said, her voice thick with excitement. They were way out of their comfort zone. He suspected they both thought that was not a bad thing.

Undressing Marcello after Tree carried him into the guest bedroom was like manipulating a rag doll. Once she got his clothes off, Freddie laid the boy on the bed and tucked covers around him. She smiled down, a beatific smile for a sleeping child, Tree thought, not unlike the one plastered on his face.

They crept from the bedroom leaving the door ajar. Freddie retreated to the kitchen for a badly needed glass of wine. Tree stripped off his clothes and stepped into the shower to relieve the tension. He emerged feeling better, but aware again of his aching hand. Otherwise, he was unscathed. Not bad for a sixty-year-old, he thought, smiling into the bathroom mirror. The insouciant action hero smiled back.

Freddie was half way through her wine when he arrived in the kitchen wearing a pair of shorts and a T-shirt. They ate leftover chicken along with a salad, seated at the kitchen table. Tree related Marcello's fears about an "operation."

"Maybe he does need an operation," Freddie said. "Maybe it's legitimate. Maybe something is wrong with him."

"If that's the case, why haven't we heard about it? Why doesn't Marcello know? Why is Mel Scott involved? Why is everyone trying to hide their involvement?"

"But if there's nothing wrong with him, why would they be operating?"

"They drugged him," Tree said. "Nobody who wants to help a child drugs him into semi-consciousness. I don't know what they were planning, but it wasn't good. Whether we're right or wrong about Marcello, he's safer with us. We don't know about these other people. That's as good a reason as I know for doing what I did."

"I'll try to remember that when we're e-mailing each other from our respective prison cells."

He carried their plates to the sink. She watched him scrape chicken bones into the recycling. "Whatever you're going to do, you'd better do it quickly, my love."

"I know."

"It won't be long before various people start to think he's here and come looking for him. How are you going to protect him then? Particularly if they've got the police on their side."

"They've got Mel Scott," he amended. "We've got Cee Jay Boone and the FBI."

"Do you?" Freddie raised an eyebrow. "Can you trust anyone?"

Good question, one Tree didn't have an answer for. Not tonight. All he knew was that, somehow, no matter what, he would protect the boy. He wasn't even sure why. He just knew he was going to protect him.

———

They awoke early and together checked the guest bedroom. Marcello lay curled on his side fast asleep, mouth slightly open, a fist pressed under his nose. They decided to leave him like that. Freddie dressed and drank the coffee Tree made for her. Then she went off to work.

At 8:30 the phone rang. It was Cee Jay Boone. "Haven't heard anything from our friend Marcello, have you?"

"Not a thing," he replied. How convincingly he had learned to tell bareface lies. He wouldn't have thought he possessed such a talent. Perhaps he should go into politics. "Why? Is there anything new?"

"Just checking in," she said. "It's been a while since we talked."

"What about our corpse?"

"Which one?"

"The one without a head."

"What about it?"

"Have you identified it yet?"

She paused too long before she said "no." He wondered if he wasn't surrounded by much more accomplished liars than himself—Cee Jay Boone, Elizabeth Traven, and Savannah Trask topped the list.

"I hear it's Dara Rait."

"Do you? Who do you hear that from?"

"Dara owned an art shop on Estero Boulevard in Fort Myers Beach. I believe she lived in an apartment above the studio. I think she lived there with Marcello. Or do you already know that?"

"I'll look into it," Cee Jay said in a neutral voice. "Thanks for the information."

"Am I a suspect?"

"A what?"

"A suspect. In Dara's murder. Or Reno O'Hara's?"

"You hear that, too?"

"Is it true?"

"Everybody's a suspect," she said and hung up.

He went down the hall and found Marcello sitting up, blinking and rubbing his eyes. "Where am I?"

"You're back at my house." Tree perched on the edge of the bed. "How are you feeling?"

"You took my letters."

"And you lied to me."

Marcello didn't say anything.

"Are you hungry?"

"Sure," he said.

Tree offered scrambled eggs and toast, not expecting Marcello to agree to such exotic fare. But for once he nodded assent.

"You know how to work the shower? Of course you do. You're a big guy, after all. Take a shower. Freddie washed your clothes last night. They're on the counter in the bathroom."

"You got my letters?"

"Take a shower. And no escaping out the window, all right?"

Tree got back a slow nod. "I want to hear you say 'yes.'"

"Okay," Marcello said.

———

By time the toast popped and the eggs were done, Marcello was dressed and in the kitchen, still sleepy-eyed. Tree put a plate in front of him. Ketchup? Marcello said yes, and even added a welcome "please." By the time Tree returned with the ketchup half the eggs were gone.

Between mouthfuls Marcello asked, "How'd I get here?"

"I brought you home last night."

"Why?"

"Because you said people were going to hurt you. You talked about an operation, and you didn't want that."

Marcello took this in without comment. He bit into another piece of toast.

"That's true, isn't it, Marcello? You were afraid those people at the house were going to hurt you?"

"They were after me," he said.

"They live in that big house on Captiva Road?"

"I don't know where they live," he said.

The telephone rang. Tree did not recognize the number on the digital display. He pick up the handset. A rumbling voice said, "Mr. Callister?"

"Yes, who is this?"

"Brand Traven calling."

Tree gripped the receiver harder. "Sorry?"

"Brand Traven. You're doing some work for my wife."

Caught off guard, Tree could only repeat, "Yes."

"I wonder if we could talk. Face to face."

"Is that possible?"

"It is if you can come up to Coleman."

When Tree didn't immediately reply, Traven rumbled again. "Mr. Callister? Are you able to do that? Could you visit me?"

Visit? Interesting way of putting it. "When would you want to do this?"

"You're a couple of hours away. Come up first thing tomorrow. I'll leave your name. You'll need photo ID. A driver's licence will do the trick. You'll also need my inmate number. Do you have a pen handy?"

"Hold on," Tree said. He glanced at Marcello. He occupied himself moving a crust of toast back and forth along the table. "How are you doing?"

Marcello shrugged and concentrated on the toast. Tree found a pen and went back to the phone.

"My number is 18331-454. Also, be careful about how you dress."

"I'm not sure what you mean."

"Avoid anything khaki. They'll think you're trying to look like an inmate and that's a no-no. Also don't wear dark clothes. They might think you're trying to impersonate a guard. For some reason they don't like Polo shirts, either. I usually advise visitors to wear a light-colored sports jacket, jeans, a light-colored shirt with an open collar. That usually does the trick."

"All right," Tree said.

"I used to read you in the *Sun-Times*. Good stuff."

"Thanks," Tree said. Flattered despite himself.

The line went dead. Tree replaced the phone on the wall. Marcello was at the counter, on his tiptoes, reaching for a box of Wheaties. Tree went over and pushed the box so that the boy could get to it.

He poured cereal into a bowl, added two per cent milk, sliced a banana into it, and placed it in front of Marcello. He frowned. "I don't like bananas."

"You don't like bananas? How can you not like bananas?"

"I don't like them."

Tree sighed and then meticulously removed the banana slices floating in the milk amid wheat flakes. He put the bowl back in front of Marcello, who now beamed.

Tree sat and watched the boy eat for a couple of moments. "I was just talking to a man on the phone."

Marcello looked at him expectantly.

"His name is Brand Traven. Does that name mean anything to you, Marcello? Brand Traven?"

Marcello looked fearful. "The Bad Man," he said.

"So you know the name."

"The Bad Man," Marcello repeated.

"Why? Why is he so bad?"

Marcello concentrated on making his spoon go in and out of the milk and cereal, fascinated by the tiny plops and splashes he produced.

"Marcello," Tree said.

The boy took a deep breath. "He made me have the operation."

He continued to play with his spoon.

"He's the Bad Man. The Bad Man."

28

The Federal Correctional Institution-Low, surrounded by chain link fences and topped with razor wire, is located outside the town of Coleman, set away from a country road between Interstate Highway 75 and the Florida turnpike. It's part of a much larger complex that includes medium and high security prisons.

Tree wore his brown-check sports jacket, jeans, his good pair of Ecco dress shoes, and the striped dress shirt he bought for his daughter's wedding. Even so, prison guards inspected him closely. He might as well have arrived with a hacksaw buried in a birthday cake.

He had to show his driver's license, fill out paperwork, take off his belt, remove his shoes, and allow himself to be marked with an ultra-violet stamp so as to ensure the inmate he was visiting didn't walk out in his place.

Most of the dozen visitors going through the same process were women, soberly dressed in anonymous sweatshirts and slacks in an effort to not offend posted instructions against provocative clothing. Everyone maintained a poker face and kept their eyes averted. If the women knew each other, they gave no indication. Tree wondered how Mickey Crowley would have managed to befriend Elizabeth Traven.

Tree and the other visitors shuffled through two sealed

rooms into a drab hall full of tables and chairs. Tree managed to find an empty table and took it just as a guard ushered Brand Traven into view.

He dressed in the uniform of prisoners at Coleman—olive green slacks and a short-sleeved olive green shirt—pausing to look around until Tree raised his arm. Traven sauntered over and said with a crooked smile, "There you are."

The tubby corporate villain of newspaper front pages and six o'clock newscasts was gone, leaving a trim and rested man in his mid-sixties, pouches beneath dead eyes, deep lines crisscrossing a high forehead.

Traven offered Tree his hand.

"Mr. Callister," he said. "Thanks for coming."

Traven sat down as a small, bald-headed man passed, hunch-shouldered, ashen-faced. He aimed a watery smile in Traven's direction. "Don't tell 'em anything, Brand."

"Don't worry, Jimmy."

As the bald-headed man moved away, Brand lowered his voice and said, "Jimmy Tragg, bush-league Madoff. Ruined widows and orphans with that oldest and least original of all frauds, the Ponzi scheme. The usual thing. Take everyone's money, say you're investing it for them, pocket their life savings, and wait for the Feds to show up at your door. Jimmy took several hundred million from despairing widows and orphans so he's cooling his heels here for the next hundred years. I'm very small potatoes compared to Jimmy."

He sat back and his voice rose. "Lots of lawyers in here. They seem particularly susceptible to greed and avarice. Also, the usual parade of bankers and businessmen. There's a former submarine commander convicted of fraud. America. Everyone's stealing something. Everyone comes to Coleman. Some do very well here." He nodded in Jimmy's direction. "Others not so well."

"Your wife says you survive, no matter what."

"Does she? Of course that's easy to say when you're not in a place like this." Traven spread his hands on the table in front of him. "I'm doing a lot of reading of Socrates. Haven't studied him since I was a kid. He's kind of like Shakespeare. Not much is actually known about Will, so you can make up any Shakespeare you like. He can be in love. He can be gay. He can even be a fraud who didn't actually write those plays. Who's to contradict you? The same is true of Socrates. Create your own Socrates, whatever suits."

"What sort of Socrates do you have in mind, Mr. Traven?"

"Plato offered a kind of saint, a god-like figure sending down philosophical decrees like thunderbolts from the heavens. I prefer the version created by Aristophanes. A clown. Aristophanes has him in a basket hanging from a rope, musing on the buzzing noise made by a gnat, advising acolytes on how to beat fraud charges."

"He would fit in nicely at Coleman."

Traven laughed. "I'm not so sure about the moralist, but the clown would, Mr. Callister. Yes, he would."

He looked over at the hulks of stainless steel vending machines lining the far wall. "Lunch, Mr. Callister? I'm afraid you'll have to buy. They don't allow us to have money."

Tree got Brand a cappuccino and a ham sandwich. He retrieved another sandwich for himself as well as a Diet Coke. They returned to their table and Brand began to extract the sandwich from its plastic wrap, his movements slow and meticulous, as though unwrapping a small bomb.

"Did you get out of the business or did they throw you out?"

"They threw me out."

"A.J. Liebling once said the function of a press in society is to inform. Its role is to make money. Alas, it no longer informs, and certainly it doesn't make money. I won't say I saw it coming but let's face it, the business has been on the downslide for years. Is it the end of newspapers? I wonder."

"Do you?"

"Some will disappear—a few are already gone—but there will be survivors. Like radio. When television came along everyone thought radio was finished. But the medium adapted, survived. A similar situation, I believe, will occur with news-papers, although not the ones with which I was associated."

"No?"

Brand laid the sandwich wrapper on the table, using the flat of his hand to smooth it.

"They say I defrauded the company, bled it dry. Yet when I gave up the chairmanship, shares traded at eight dollars. Now they're down to seventy-eight cents. The company is worthless. The people who were supposed to save it ended up destroying it and raping shareholders in the bargain. They say I lined my pockets. What about these charlatans? They've pilfered hundreds of millions of dollars in unearned fees and no one says anything. But then I suppose everyone in this room can do a variation on my speech. You should hear Jimmy Tragg go on about how he was victimized by the government."

"Were you victimized?"

His grin widened. "Well, that's my story isn't it? This place is filled with the innocent. I feel right at home."

"You're just more innocent than the rest," Tree said.

"I like to think so." No grin this time.

"Is that why I'm here? To help you prove your innocence?"

"Or perhaps a prisoner without a lot of visitors just needs an interesting conversation from time to time. Whatever I may think of journalists, they do make great talkers."

Traven raised his eyebrows as though to cue interesting conversation from Tree.

"I haven't been a journalist for a while," he said.

"Then perhaps curiosity brings us together."

"Whose curiosity? Yours or mine?"

"I'm curious as to why—or I suppose the better word is how—how a man of your obvious talents ends up on a small island in the Gulf of Mexico, anonymous and forgotten, pursuing detective work of all things."

Tree said, "The Socrates you talk about is from the play by Aristophanes titled *The Clouds*. At the end, the intellectual brilliance of Socrates, his terrible arrogant belief in his own omnipotence, is defeated by the rabble rising against him."

Traven stared a long moment before he produced something approximating a smile. "Dear me, Mr. Callister, I hope we're not all misjudging you."

"I wouldn't worry about that," Tree said.

"But when it comes down to it, Socrates aside, we're both in the same boat."

"No, we're not. I'm on a lovely island in the sun. You're sitting in a jail cell."

"I didn't mean to anger you, Mr. Callister," Traven said.

"No, of course not."

"And I do not deride your new profession. To the contrary. I hope to make use of it."

He leaned forward. "I have a small, closely knit group around me. My wife, obviously, a few others. I would like you to be part of that group."

"Your wife fired me."

"Have you read any of her books?"

"The Stalin. Years ago."

"The secret of my wife, Mr. Callister, I believe she's actually quite enamored of communism. She writes continually of those who corrupted its ideals, but the philosophy itself, what Marx originally espoused, I think she is a believer. A disappointed believer, but a believer."

"Married to a jailed capitalist."

Traven spent more time looking at his hands. "Anyway, I'm rehiring you."

"To do what?"

"Continue your work. Help my wife with security, especially when it comes to this woman."

"Mickey Crowley?"

"Yes."

"And her husband, Dwayne."

"Dwayne Crowley is here."

"Is he?"

"Unless you know something I don't."

"What about Reno O'Hara?"

"What about him?"

"Was he part of your group?"

"Reno did some work for me."

"What kind of work?"

"Do you mean did he do anything illegal? No, he did not. However, I would be lying if I said I didn't know something of his background."

"The work he did for you, did that include coming to my office to threaten me?"

Traven looked taken aback. "No, of course not. I'm not trying to scare you, Mr. Callister, I'm trying to hire you to help us."

"If you were interested in finding Reno's boy, Marcello, for example, I might be able to help you there."

Traven's eyes narrowed. "Yes, provided, of course, we were looking for the boy."

"For the operation."

Traven picked his next words carefully. "What operation, Mr. Callister?"

"I thought Marcello needed an operation, and you are helping him with it."

"I know my wife is concerned about the young fellow's well-being," Traven said with studied smoothness. "Our first priority would be to locate him, ascertain what his needs are, and decide how we can help him."

"You know the FBI is looking for him?"

Traven paused longer than he should have before he said, "I didn't know the FBI was involved."

"They are."

"Twenty thousand dollars, Mr. Callister."

Tree looked at him.

"Is that enough?" Brand Traven asked.

"False words are not only evil in themselves," Tree said, "but they infect the soul with evil."

"And that is?"

"Socrates," Tree said.

Brand Traven frowned at his uneaten sandwich. "You'll have your money by eleven o'clock tomorrow morning."

29

Had he been bought? Tree thought as he drove south along I-75 toward Fort Myers.

He supposed he had—or would be, as soon as he had twenty thousand dollars in his hands. He always had wondered what it would be like to be bribed, tempted—*corrupted*. Rather matter-of-fact, it turned out, dressed up as a simple business transaction. Tree could see how Brand Traven might have done the same with his media empire. It's business so I'll just skim a few million out of the till and stick it in my pocket. Well, Tree Callister was a long way from a few million. He could be had for a measly twenty thousand dollars.

"What was Traven like?" Freddie asked after he got home that evening. She had spent the day with Marcello, uneventful, she said. Except they had a lot of fun together.

"He talked about Socrates."

"You must have felt right at home."

"If you get a good wife, you'll become happy. If you get a bad one, you become a philosopher."

"Where did that come from?"

"Socrates."

Freddie looked impressed—fleetingly. "From Traven?"

Tree shook his head. "When I fed him Socrates he didn't recognize the quote."

"Is that a fact?"

"And when I launched into a bunch of meaningless gibberish about a play called *The Clouds* in which Socrates makes an appearance, Traven bought right into it."

"Which is to say what? Anyone who really did know the play or Socrates never would have swallowed it?"

"Not for a moment."

"Maybe he was just trying to be polite."

"Traven doesn't strike you as a man who feels an overwhelming need to be polite."

"So he's full of shit?"

"Or a man not telling the truth about any number of things."

"I think they know we have the boy," she said. "Or they strongly suspect."

"That's a distinct possibility."

"They've threatened you, and broken into the house, and none of that has worked. So the question they must be asking is, What will work?"

"Money," Tree said.

"Exactly. Cue your new Socrates-loving friend Brand Traven."

"He even likes the way I write."

"Flattery won't work, either."

"It won't?"

"You can't be bought."

"I can't?" Tree said. "You're sure about that?"

"I am."

"I'm not."

"Yes, you are. You're incorruptible. That's what I love about you. You are as honest as the day is long."

"Twenty thousand dollars could shorten the day considerably. Particularly when the guy bribing me compliments my writing."

"You would turn Marcello over for a measly twenty thousand dollars?"

"Well, I would need a compliment or two to go along with it."

"Tree."

"Maybe it's a lifetime of being underpaid in the newspaper business, but twenty thousand dollars is not my idea of measly."

"You haven't answered my question. Would you turn him over or not?"

"Not even if he likes the way I write."

"Then you really are the man I married." Freddie yawned. "Being with a child all day is tiring, let me tell you."

"So is hanging out in federal prisons. Also, there is something I forgot to tell you."

She looked at him. "About being happily married in the Socratic sense?"

"Not about that."

"The fact that one of the FBI agents is your old girlfriend?"

Tree stared in dumb amazement. "Most days you just surprise me," he said. "Some days, though, some days you *really* surprise me. How did you know?"

"Could be that you're not the only detective in the house," she said impishly. "Or it could be Detective Cee Jay Boone called looking for you and accidentally spilled the beans."

"You're not mad?"

"I may well be mad," Freddie said. "Am I angry? No."

"Why not?" Did he sound somewhat indignant?

"You're going to run away with some chick you lived with twenty years ago?"

"Stranger things have happened."

"Besides, it takes two to tango."

"How do you know Savannah doesn't want to run off with me?"

"Because she dumped you. Now she takes one look at you and wants you back? I don't think so."

"That's rather brutal."

"Not brutal at all, my love. Just realistic."

"What makes you so sure I didn't leave her?"

"Incidentally, are you happy or a philosopher?"

Tree thought about it. "Well, I'm no philosopher."

Freddie leaned over and brushed his lips with hers. "Good answer."

"You haven't answered my question."

She gave him a delicious smile before she breezed away. The phone rang.

"Mr. Callister?" It was Tommy Dobbs. Tree groaned.

"Mr. Callister, I need your help." Tommy's voice was slurry and scared. "I'm in awful trouble."

30

Nemo's poked onto the beach beneath a gold-colored canvas marquee. The usual LCD monitors showed the usual football games to a clientele more interested in the drama unfolding near a wall poster listing fifteen reasons why a beer is better than a woman, including "a beer doesn't get jealous when you have another beer."

Tommy Dobbs, backed against the bar, swung an empty beer stein in the general direction of the three men closing in on him. His white face glistened in the yellowish light. The light transformed the bruise on his right cheek into an India ink smear. Despite the damage to his face, he still managed to retain his Ray-Bans.

"Hey, Tommy," Tree said.

"Mr. Callister, I never thought you'd come." Tommy sounded out of breath.

"What are you up to?" Tree had to raise his voice to compete with the hard rock blues of ZZ Top.

"He's about to get himself killed," said the biggest of the three, showing a blotchy face and bushy beard beneath a Florida Marlins baseball cap. Tattoos crawled up his thick forearms. The other two, bare-headed, also wore their tattoos where you could see them. Not the sort of hombres you wanted to piss off in a shitkicker bar late at night. But that's exactly what Tommy appeared to have done.

"Come on, Tommy, time to go home."

"This clown ain't goin' nowhere, except to the hospital," said the tallest and skinniest of the three. He hadn't shaved for a couple of days.

"Leave me alone," Tommy said in a strangled voice.

"He's drunk and harmless," Tree said.

"He's drunk and an asshole," the skinny guy shot back.

In the background Dolly Parton's dreamy country romanticism replaced Billy Gibbons' fine guitar riffs. It didn't seem to change anybody's attitude.

"Got a big mouth on him," Bushy Beard said.

"He does at that," Tree said agreeably. "Let me get him out of here."

Tommy regarded Tree with bleary sadness. "I'm so happy you're here, Mr. Callister."

"What are you, his old man or something?" The guy with the beard.

"Just a friend." Tree removed the beer glass from Tommy's hand. Tommy seemed barely aware he was giving it up.

The third guy, greasy black hair pushed back from a pimply forehead, raised a meaty fist. Bushy Beard caught the fist in his hand. "Not worth it," he said. The Greasy-Haired Guy's eyes flashed. Bushy Beard gave him a hard look. The Greasy-Haired Guy backed off.

Tommy sagged. Tree managed to catch him before he hit the floor.

"I shouldn't be here," Tommy mumbled.

"No, you shouldn't." Tree hoisted Tommy away from the bar. He caught the eye of the guy with the bushy beard. "Thanks."

"Tell your friend not to come back."

"I don't think you have to worry about that," Tree said.

Tree half carried, half dragged Tommy along a cinderblock corridor past a replica of a vintage red Corvette mounted on the wall. He got him onto Estero Boulevard and across the street to where he had parked the Beetle. He propped Tommy against the side of the car, trying to find his key.

"Why don't you like me, Mr. Callister?"

"Who says I don't like you, Tommy?" Tree found his key and unlocked the door.

"You don't like me 'cause I'm a loser."

"Tommy, get in the car," Tree said. "I'm driving you home."

"Don't you?" Tommy was more vehement.

"I think you're young," he said. "In a business I don't recognize any more. You want me to be things I don't think I can be."

"I want you to be my friend." A note of desperation.

Tree looked at him, at a loss for words.

"Can't you be my friend, Mr. Callister? Is that so hard for you? To be my friend?"

Tree put his hand on Tommy's shoulder. "Sure, Tommy," he said. "I can be your friend."

Tommy threw up on the Beetle.

My pal Tommy, Tree thought.

————

The next morning Freddie, summery in a pink floral print, came into the kitchen where Tree was pouring coffee. He handed her a cup.

"I'm not sure if you're aware of it, but there's someone with pimples sleeping on our couch."

"That's reporter Tommy Dobbs. My biggest fan."

"I thought I was your biggest fan."

"You are my biggest fan without pimples. At least, I hope you are."

"Never doubt it, pal."

"You should have seen me last night. I took on a room full of drunk barflies."

"My hero," she said.

"I can't believe I did it."

"Life lately is filled with things you can't believe you did," Freddie observed.

Yes it is, Tree thought. Yes, it is.

After Freddie went to work, Tree poured more coffee and took it into the living room. In the car after he threw up, Tommy had promptly passed out. Tree decided to bring him home. Just like the old days, dragging drunk reporters back to the house in the middle of the night. Didn't his first wife just love that. Tommy lay on his back, still wearing the Ray-Bans, his pale face glistening like the polished death mask of a boy pharaoh.

Tree perched on the edge of the couch. Tommy awakened with a lip-smacking grunt, sitting bolt upright.

"I feel awful," he said.

Tree offered him the coffee.

"Can't even look at it."

"Suit yourself." Tree sipped the coffee. "So what did you do to piss those guys off?"

"Not sure," Tommy said.

"What were you doing there in the first place?"

"Don't know. Can't remember much."

"Bathroom's down the hall." Tree got to his feet. "Get yourself cleaned up and I'll drive you home."

Tommy held his head at an angle. "Gotta go to work."

"All right. Take a shower. I'll get you a towel."

Tommy looked up at Tree with unhappy, bloodshot eyes. "I'm sorry, Mr. Callister."

"Happens to the best of us."

"I'll bet it never happened to you."

"Long ago, in a galaxy far, far away," Tree said.

An hour later, Tree parked in front of the *Island Reporter*'s office. Tommy looked as though he had just climbed out of a sarcophagus.

"I really appreciate what you did for me," he said.

"It took me a long time to learn this but it's something to keep in mind: Ernest Hemingway is dead."

Tommy looked befuddled. "I'm not very familiar with Hemingway."

Tree shook his head. "Get out of the car, Tommy."

31

Tree got to his office at ten thirty—half an hour before Brand Traven's messenger was due to arrive with twenty thousand dollars. The prospect did not excite him. Freddie was right. What was twenty thousand dollars in the scheme of things? More money than he earned in a year? He tried not to think about that.

He went toward the back stairs and encountered Rex Baxter on his way down. "I just saw a ghost," Rex said.

"You're spending too much time in the bar at the Lighthouse," Tree said.

"Savannah," Rex said.

"She's upstairs?"

"She's an FBI agent." Rex made it sound as though she had landed on the moon.

"I know that, Rex."

"What's she doing in town?"

"Unless I miss my guess, she thinks I killed someone."

"You? Killing someone? Get serious. She lived with you for God's sake."

"Maybe that was her first clue."

"Weird thing is, she hasn't changed. There's a portrait of her in a closet somewhere that's getting old, but not her. It's like I always figured. She's in league with the devil."

"You never did like her, Rex."

"Does Freddie know she's in town?"

"Freddie knows everything."

"My advice? Do not go up there. Stay away till she flies out of town on her broomstick."

"I'm a big boy. I can handle this."

"Where Savannah is concerned, all bets are off."

Tree took a deep breath and mounted the stairs two at a time. FBI Agent Savannah Trask sat in his chair holding a Starbucks Grande Caffe Latte. Another latte waited on his desk.

"You wear glasses," she said.

"Only for reading," Tree replied, removing the telltale specs, kicking himself for forgetting to get rid of them before he entered the office.

"I just saw, Rex."

"I know. He thinks you're a ghost."

"He probably thinks I'm flying around on a broomstick."

"He doesn't think you've changed since Chicago."

"He never did like me."

"Why do you suppose that is?"

"He probably thinks I broke your heart or something. He certainly loves your latest wife."

"Everyone loves Freddie."

"That sounds like the title of a sitcom. Are you all right?"

"A little surprised to find the FBI in my office first thing in the morning, that's all."

He reached for the coffee.

"I hope you don't mind," she said.

"Mind?" He wrestled with the plastic top. He never could get the damned things off, and he hated drinking through that little hole.

"The door was open." She watched him defeated by the plastic coffee top.

"You're always welcome, Savannah," he said as amiably as he could. "Particularly when you bring coffee." He still couldn't get the top off.

"Do you need help with that?"

"With what?"

"The coffee."

"No of course not." He delivered what he considered a disarming grin.

The lid popped off. Foam spilled over the rim and rolled down the side of the cup. He said a silent prayer of thanks and sipped at his coffee, managing to glance at his watch. Less than half an hour. Tree felt a tightening in his stomach.

"Have I come at a bad time?"

"Why would you say that?"

She pointed an accusatory finger. "You've got some foam there."

"Where?"

"At the corner of your mouth."

He brushed at his mouth.

"That's better."

He drank more coffee. It was lukewarm. She watched him carefully, as though anticipating another misstep.

"So Tree, what were you doing up at Coleman yesterday?"

"News travels fast."

"Tell me."

"I was seeing a potential client."

"You're kidding me. Brand Traven is a client?"

"Potential. If you already know this stuff, why are you bothering to ask me?"

"Because I no sooner tell you confidentially that Mr. Traven is a subject of interest to us than you scoot up to Coleman to meet with him."

"I didn't scoot up there," Tree said.

"Nonetheless, it looks damned suspicious."

Just wait until someone shows up with a bag full of money, Tree thought. The tightening in his stomach increased.

"Traven called me, I didn't call him."

"Why would he do that? How does he even know you?"

"I've done some work for his wife."

"You're working for Elizabeth Traven?" She was trying to keep surprise hidden behind a veneer of professionalism and not doing a good job. "What kind of work?"

"Protection," he said.

She scrutinized him, perhaps getting used to the idea that Tree might be able to protect anyone.

"From what? What does Elizabeth Traven need protection from?"

"She is concerned about a female acquaintance. She asked me to look into the woman's background."

"Don't tell me the female is Mickey Crowley."

"It is."

"What? Brand Traven wants you to protect him, too?"

"You know, it could turn out I'm working with you, not against you."

"Could it turn out that way, Tree? Be nice if it did." Her voice softened. "I hate the idea of putting old boyfriends in jail. Some old boyfriends. Rex would never forgive me."

Savannah put her empty cup on the desk. "You know how I think of you, Tree?"

"I don't have a clue," Tree said. As honest a statement as he had made this morning.

"I think of you as a sweet, naïve guy out of my youthful past."

"Sweet and naïve? Is that what you thought?"

"Yes."

"Savannah, you were twenty-two. How practiced in the world do you think you were?"

She smiled. "Precisely why I thought you were naïve."

"The word is trusting."

She shrugged. "Whatever. I think of you in a certain way, a guy playing at something with no idea what he's got himself into. On the other hand—"

"On the other hand?"

"Maybe I'm wrong about you. Maybe you're not so naïve."

"Why would the Travens be interested in Marcello?" Tree said

"Are they?"

"Let's suppose they are."

"I was hoping you could tell me."

He finished his coffee. "That was very good," he said. "Hit the spot first thing in the morning."

"What's that? Your way of saying you're not going to tell me anything?"

"No, it's my way of saying that we need a little tit for tat here. You give me something, and I give you something back."

"Tree, this isn't some boy-girl game we're playing, trying to recapture lost youth. If you've got Marcello and you're not telling us, or the Travens have the boy and you're not telling us, then that's lying to a federal officer, and that's not a good thing."

"Sounds like we're right back to threatening boyfriends," he said.

"And you know I wouldn't want to do that—with most old boyfriends."

"How many are there, anyway?"

He got one of her enigmatic smiles. "Let's stick to the subject—the pitfalls of lying to federal officers."

"What about local police officers?"

"You can't lie to them, either."

"What I mean is, how do you feel about them?"

She curled an eyebrow. "What are you getting at?"

"Do you trust them?"

A couple of telling beats before she said, "Why shouldn't I trust them?"

"One of the reasons Marcello keeps running away, he's afraid of the police."

"Why would he be afraid of them?"

"Maybe because they're mixed up in this in ways they shouldn't be."

"If you know something Tree, you should tell me."

"Because you don't know anything?"

She rose to her feet. "Here's what I'm going to do. I'm

going to give you until the end of the week to come up with the boy."

"Or you send your pal Shawn around to kick the shit out of me? Is that it?"

"What?"

"The other night when I left your place, he jumped me in the parking lot."

"You're not serious."

"He told me to stay away from you."

"I don't believe it." But for the first time she appeared uncertain.

"Yes, you do, Savannah. You're involved with him. Or he thinks he's involved with you, and he's jealous of me."

She actually looked rattled for a moment. Then she regained the poise of a professional law enforcement officer facing a hostile witness. "One week."

"I think Shawn would like that, kicking the shit out of me."

She went out slamming the door behind her.

32

Tree looked at his watch.

Eleven o'clock. An accident of timing? Or a sign of his increasing ability to manage deceit? There was something deeply satisfying about lying. Perhaps that's why everyone did it so enthusiastically. Telling the truth didn't require much art. Lying, covering up, saying one thing, intending something else entirely—all that demanded real talent.

He looked out the window as Savannah crossed the parking lot and Elizabeth Traven got out of her car wearing a tailored suit; the sleek corporate executive on her way to a morning meeting. She reached into the back seat for a valise that she then carried toward the entrance.

Savannah reached her car before turning abruptly to watch Elizabeth enter the building. Then she looked up at Tree. Instinctively, he ducked back—and immediately felt embarrassed.

He listened to the click of Elizabeth's high heels coming up the stairs. She entered wearing the expression of an unhappy rich man's wife about to part with money. She dropped the valise to the floor as if she could not be bothered with it any more.

"That was an FBI agent," she said in an accusatory voice.

"Yes, it was," he said. "Her name is Savannah Trask."

"What was she doing here?"

"Wondering what I was doing up at Coleman talking to your husband."

"This was supposed to remain confidential."

"Confidentiality went out the window as soon as I walked into the prison."

She heaved a sigh before dropping into the now familiar office chair.

"What did you tell the FBI?"

"I tried not to tell them too much of anything, but they know something is up."

"What exactly?"

"They know Reno O'Hara worked for your husband."

Elizabeth's flawlessly constructed features showed nothing.

Tree went on. "They are trying to link him to Reno's murder, and you, too, I suppose."

"That's ridiculous," she countered. "My husband's in jail. He's hardly in a position to murder people. I haven't knocked anyone off in years."

"Like just about everyone on the island, they want to know where Marcello is."

"Do you know?"

"Do I know what?"

"Quit playing games," she said impatiently. "Do you know the whereabouts of Marcello O'Hara?"

"The FBI thinks I know more than I'm telling them."

"Do you?"

"I'm not sure I do," he said truthfully. "For instance, I don't know why you and your husband are so interested in the boy."

Elizabeth opened the valise and extracted a package wrapped in brown paper. She might have been delivering his laundry. The thought made him smile. "What's so funny?"

"Nothing," he said.

"I wonder what you are up to, Mr. Callister." She laid the package on his desk.

"The FBI said the same thing. Everyone wants to know what I'm up to. Everyone thinks I know something."

"Mind if I give you some advice?"

"Go ahead, Mrs. Traven. Everyone seems to be handing it out this morning."

"So far you've been fortunate. Don't overplay your hand. No one's going to get hurt here if everyone does what they are supposed to do."

"What am I supposed to do?" Tree said.

"Take your money," she said brusquely. "The rest is up to you, isn't it?"

"Yes, I suppose it is."

"I'll be waiting for your call."

Elizabeth Traven on her way out did not slam the door quite so hard as Savannah.

The package was sealed with Scotch tape. There was no bow. He tore at the paper. Bundles of twenty dollar bills tumbled across his desk. Tree stared at the money.

Not even noon yet and he had been threatened by two beautiful women and collected twenty thousand dollars. Not bad, he thought. Not bad at all.

———

Freddie, in a one-piece orange bathing suit that did wonderful things to the shape of her, was in the pool with Marcello when Tree got back to the house. She had objected only mildly when he asked if she could stay with the boy for a couple of hours. She knew full well why he was going into the office, but to his surprise and relief, chose not to argue about it.

Tree found a chair in the shade. He sat with the package on his lap. Freddie lifted herself out of the pool, grabbed a towel and settled into an adjacent chair so she could keep an eye on Marcello. He flopped onto an inflatable cushion wearing a pair of oversize sunglasses.

"You two look like you're having a good time," Tree observed.

"He's a terrific kid, he really is." Her eyes danced. "You

know, he plays it so close to the chest, you forget sometimes he's a little boy."

"He is that," Tree agreed.

"Ray called me."

"The Ray Man. Did he fire you?"

"He apologized."

"Interesting. I would have thought he owes me the apology."

"He says he doesn't remember anything."

"Convenient."

"He's worried that I didn't go in. He thinks I'm pissed."

"Did he even mention me?"

"I told him I wasn't coming in for a while. Not until I figure out a few things."

"He didn't. Bastard."

She eyed the package on his lap. "Okay, I give up. What happened?"

"I got the money."

"I can see that. Delivered right to your door."

"I suddenly realize I'm not quite sure what to do with twenty thousand possibly ill-gotten dollars."

"How about not accepting them in the first place?"

"If I stick it in the bank, the FBI will know about it. So what do you do? Hide it under the mattress?"

"Tree, did you hear me?"

"Now I know how Mexican drug lords must feel. You've got all this money, but what do you do with it?"

"Tree."

"I'm not compromising anything, Freddie."

"You are if you're being paid to turn that boy over to them."

"Not necessarily."

"I'm not going to let you do it," Freddie said.

"You're the one who wanted to take him to the police—remember?"

She watched Marcello floating in the pool. "He brings out the mothering instinct in me." She glanced at him. "Not an instinct I've experienced for a while."

"It looks good on you," Tree said. "Makes you more adorable."

"Don't try to butter me up. I said before I wasn't sure I liked this new Tree, the Sanibel Sunset Detective Tree. I'm even less certain now."

"Because I'm earning some money?"

"You bring lots of things to the marriage, Tree. You don't have to bring money. I can get that."

"The FBI was waiting when I got to the office this morning."

She peered at him with narrowing eyes. "You mean your former live-in girlfriend Savannah Trask. What did she want?"

"She gave me the rest of the week to come up with Marcello. Or else."

"How does she look?"

"I tell you I've been threatened by a federal agent and your response is 'How does she look?'"

"Answer the question."

"Rex thinks she's a ghost because she hasn't changed since Chicago."

"I don't believe it. Everybody changes."

"After Savannah left, Elizabeth Traven showed up."

"With the money? That must have been interesting."

"She obviously doesn't like her husband's interference—and she's expecting me to turn over the boy. Or else."

"The point being?"

"The point being whether I take money or not we don't have much more time. We've got to decide what to do, and do it fast."

"So what's the plan, Sherlock?"

"Find his mother. That's what I've been paid for. That's what I'm going to do."

Marcello came over, dripping wet, still wearing the oversize sunglasses. Freddie wrapped a towel around him. It seemed like a protective gesture.

"Let's do something," Marcello said.

"What would you like to do?"

He shrugged. "I'm kind of bored."

"Oh, dear," Freddie said with a grin. "We can't have that, can we?"

"All I do is hang around. Even school's better than this."

Freddie and Tree traded glances.

School?

Tree asked, "Where do you go to school, Marcello?"

"Heights," he promptly answered.

"Heights what?"

"Heights Elementary School," he said.

Tree started for the house. "Where are you going?" Freddie asked.

"To get my camera."

"Camera? What do you need a camera for?"

"So I can take a photo of Marcello," he said.

33

The yellow umbrellas and the picnic-type tables in front of Heights Elementary did a nice job of diverting attention from the institutional look of the building. Tree parked the Beetle in the lot at the side, still kicking himself for being so stupid. Of course, the kid would go to school, and of course that might be the key to who he was, and where he lived, and who his parents were.

Of course.

Inside, Tree's footsteps echoed along empty hallways, the children behind closed doors hard at work becoming tomorrow's leaders. Tree found the front office. A sign on the wall read, "Reaching new heights; climbing the ladder of success."

"Our school motto." The woman behind the counter removed fashionable eyeglasses for a better look at him. "What can I do for you, sir? Are you here about one of the students?"

Tree took out his digital camera, adjusted the LCD screen until it displayed his photo of Marcello. "His name's Marcello O'Hara. I'm wondering if he's a student here."

The woman frowned at the photo. "I think you had better talk to our principal, Mrs. Salter."

The woman disappeared through a door at the back of the office. A couple of minutes later, she re-emerged followed by an authoritative-looking black woman in a dark pantsuit.

"Good morning," she said in the no-nonsense tone he had not heard since high school. "I'm Mrs. Salter."

Tree introduced himself and showed her the photo of Marcello. Mrs. Salter studied it longer than the woman behind the counter, then she too frowned. "What did you say his name was?"

"Marcello O'Hara," Tree said.

"That's not the name we have him registered under. We know him as Gregory Scott. He hasn't been at school for a couple of weeks now. We've been worried about him and have been trying to get in touch with his father."

"Who is his father?"

"A Mr. Mel Scott."

Tree couldn't believe what he was hearing. "The police detective? Mel Scott?"

"I don't know what Mr. Scott does for a living."

"And what about his mother?"

"I don't know that we have a mother for Gregory. A stepmother. Dara Rait. We haven't been able to get hold of either Mr. Scott or his partner. I even drove over to Dara's studio a few days ago."

"On Estero?"

"Yes, but there was no one there." Her eyes narrowed. "What is your interest in this, sir? Are you a member of the family?"

"I'm a detective," he said. "I've been hired to find the boy's mother."

"Well, I'm afraid I can't help you there. Can't you talk to Mr. Scott about this?"

"Yes, I certainly intend to," Tree said.

"What did you say your name was?"

"Callister. Tree Callister."

"Mr. Callister, let's go into my office." In the same voice that used to give him detentions.

He started backing away. "I'm late for another appointment, Mrs. Salter. I'll be in touch."

The school principal transformed into a drill sergeant whose orders weren't being obeyed. "Sir!"

"Thanks for your help."

She called to him again as he exited the office. He hurried along the empty hall, half expecting Mrs. Salter to tackle him, delighted to defy school authority after so many years.

———

Tree pulled into a Winn Dixie parking lot off Gladiolus and made a phone call.

"Detective Boone."

"It's Tree Callister."

"I was just thinking about you." Suggesting that was not good.

"I have to see you," Tree said.

"You have to see me. Okay. Come into the office."

"No," Tree said. "Lighthouse Beach in forty minutes—and you come alone."

Tree hung up before she could object. A white van, its side displaying a body outlined in black, pulled up beside him. Todd Jackson waved. Tree turned off his engine and got out of the car. Todd rolled down his window hitting Tree with a blast of Johnny Cash and cold air.

Todd said, "Everything all right?"

"I pulled in to make a phone call," Tree said. "What are you up to?"

"Just coming back from a job in Bonita Springs. How are you holding up?"

"I'm okay."

"What about Freddie? How's she doing?"

"She's okay, too."

"You know, given the circumstances."

"What circumstances are you talking about, Todd?'"

"Her walking out on that son-of-a-bitch, Ray."

"What?"

"Shit, I don't blame you for hitting the guy. Still, I guess it makes it pretty tough on Freddie. I mean you punch out someone's boss, what do you do?"

"What exactly do you mean by walking out?"

Todd looked confused. "Well, quitting. Freddie quit her job. Didn't she?"

"How do you know this?"

"I dunno, Tree. I mean how can you not know? Everybody knows. It's all over town."

———

Incoming clouds reduced the sun to a yellow haze. A few brave souls faced down the breakers rolling in on the beach. Three little boys in floppy sun hats knelt over a crumbling sandcastle. A large man with a small dog passed the lighthouse.

Tree recalled playing on this beach as a kid. A long time ago, but as near as yesterday. He slumped on the sand, staring at the gunmetal sea. You could view a lifetime from here, the years spreading across the water, everything clear and easily reviewed for their shortcomings and failures. Where had he gone from here? What had he done? What did it mean when you found yourself right back at the same spot where you more or less started?

Except he was no longer starting anything. He was verging on old age if he wasn't there already. The fact that he could lay out most of his life sitting here on this beach was testament to that.

Then it hit him. That's where he had seen those letters. They were as close as his past. Right there in front of him, as the past tended to be these days.

He stood and checked his watch. Cee Jay Boone was late. He would have left except the detective chose that moment to emerge from the parking lot.

"Sorry," she said, shielding her eyes from the sun's glare for a better view of him. "Something at the office I had to take care of."

She pulled a pack of Camels from her shoulder purse and shoved one into her mouth, turning against the wind coming off the gulf, cupping her hand over the cigarette while she used a Bic to light it.

"You look a little tense, Tree. Everything all right?"

Tree watched her inhale. "Why did I think you didn't smoke?"

"For five years I didn't," she said. "I started again a week or so ago."

"Why would you do that?"

"I don't know. The pressure of police work? That's as good an excuse as any, I guess. Maybe we're both a little tense these days."

"You never know about people," he said.

"Are you just now learning that, Tree? You're late to the party."

"You could be right. For instance, I'm just learning about Mel Scott."

While her right hand held the cigarette, she again employed her left hand as a sun shield.

"You know, Mel and Michelle Crowley."

She lowered her hand and said, "What about them?"

"I saw them coming down a flight of stairs together. Mel was holding Marcello."

Cee Jay didn't say anything. She took a long drag on her cigarette.

"I was hoping for a snappier comeback," he said.

"I'm trying to decide whether I can trust you."

"Over at Heights Elementary where Marcello is registered as Gregory Scott, they think Mel is his father. Dara's the stepmother, according to the principal. Interesting combination, don't you think?"

"Interesting is not the word I would use when talking about Mel."

"Yeah? What word should I use talking about you?"

"Trustworthy," Cee Jay said.

"So then help me out."

"Here's the deal. Mel's working this thing undercover," Cee Jay said. "His relationship with Dara was part of that. She's been raising Marcello the last couple of years. When it came to time register him at Heights, I guess for some reason they thought it better to use that name."

"Mel's working undercover? What for?"

"Dara was a body parts dealer, running a posse out of Mexico. These are the people Mel and I are after."

"A body parts dealer? What the hell is that?"

Cee Jay flicked more ashes. "You need a kidney? Tissues? Organs? A heart, even. Dara could get it for you. Big business these days. Reno and Dara were partners. Mel says they weren't getting along. Reno was out of control, attracting too much attention, including your friend at the FBI. He was afraid Dara might give him up. So he dealt with it the way Reno deals with problems—he cut off Dara's head."

"Then who killed Reno?"

Cee Jay dropped the remainder of the cigarette to the sand and ground it out with her heel.

"You're Reno O'Hara. You're a scumbag. You make enemies on both sides of the border. Lots of competition in the body parts business these days. The number of candidates is endless."

The sun broke free of the low-hanging cloud cover drenching the sky in crimson. Then the clouds swallowed up the escaping light, and it grew darker.

"Looks like rain," Cee Jay said. She shifted her eyes to Tree. "I'm being honest with you, Tree. Now I need you to be honest with me."

"Okay."

"Tell me where Marcello is."

When Tree didn't respond, Cee Jay said, "You have to trust me, Tree. Okay? Mel and I can protect Marcello from Mickey Crowley and her pals, but first we need to know where he is."

"Give me until tomorrow."

"You're cutting it close here, Tree. Dwayne Crowley is out of prison. They are desperate to get hold of the boy. Better if you give him up now."

"I know where he is, but it's going to take me until tomorrow to get him," Tree said.

"Tomorrow. No tricks."

"You're sure about Mel?"

"As sure as I am about anything," Cee Jay said. "Can I count on you or not, Tree?"

"Looks like we'll have to count on each other, Cee Jay."

"Just be careful. Dwayne is a whole bunch worse than Reno when it comes to being a homicidal son of a bitch."

Cee Jay headed back to the parking lot. He could see her trying to light another cigarette a moment before she disappeared. Out in the gulf, lightning stitched against the darkening clouds. The sky turned velvety black. Tree stood in the wind.

———

Freddie wasn't in the house when he got home and neither was the boy. He remembered she was taking him over to the mall for a haircut. He went into the garage, to the cabinet in the corner Freddie had been after him to clean out—the battered repository for his messy past.

He searched his pockets until he found his reading glasses. He opened the top drawer and began flipping through file folders and old photo albums, the collected evidence of failed marriages and past lives, barely recognizable faces in fading Kodak colors. Yellowed newspaper clippings recounted nearly-forgotten stories—an obit of Richard Burton he barely remembered writing. A *Cosmopolitan* magazine profile about Michael Douglas, anonymously rewritten to make him sound like a giddy young thing, madly infatuated with Michael. Why had he held onto that?

He found a dog-eared photograph of him with actor William Hurt. Hurt looked as though he would rather be anywhere else in the world. A publicity shot of a bathing suit model he briefly dated. More photos. Ex-wives looking happier than they were; children looking sadder.

And finally, what he was searching for. The letter.

My love
I don't know how it is two people who get along as well as we basically do, get into fights like this. Am I just being im-

mature? I don't know. I don't know about us sometimes, except I do. When I think about us, I think about loving you, because, dear Tree, I do love you. We never discuss the subject, but there it is; I love you. Does that surprise you? It shouldn't. We are together after all, even when we fight. I know you don't want me away this weekend, but it is only for the weekend, and I will be thinking of you.

And how much I love you.

S

After all this time the words still haunted and stung. But he didn't want to think about that. The words were beside the point now. He took the letter into his office, unlocked the top drawer of his desk, and took out the blue cards from Marcello's mom. He laid them beside the letter from Savannah.

The handwriting was the same. As he knew it would be.

His cell phone buzzed.

"I need to see you," said the voice of Elizabeth Traven.

34

Rain, unaccustomed rain, poured down on Sanibel-Captiva. The Beetle's windshield wipers were helpless against the onslaught. The little car shuddered and shook in the wind, like an old dog afraid of the storm. Tree leaned over the wheel, trying to see the road in front of him. He pulled onto the shoulder and called Freddie.

"We just got in," Freddie said. "Were you here?"

"A few minutes ago," Tree said.

"Where are you now?"

"On my way to Elizabeth Traven's."

A pause before Freddie said, "Is that a good idea?"

"I'm not sure what is or is not a good idea at this point. I'm a little concerned about what's happening. Can you get Marcello out of there for the time being?"

"You think that's necessary?"

"Humor me, okay? At least for tonight, until I get to the bottom of a couple of things."

"Go to the police, Tree."

"I've just been talking to the police. I'm not sure how helpful they are going to be. For now I'd feel better if you weren't at the house."

"I guess I could take him over to Jill Stone's place. She's one of the assistant managers."

"Did you quit your job?"

"Who told you that?"

"Apparently it's all over the island."

"I didn't realize I was so famous."

"Freddie."

"Ray's been on the phone. We've talked. I'm not sure what I've done. Right now, I'd better get Marcello out of here. We can talk about this later. I love you."

"I love you, too."

"Please, please, Tree. Please be careful."

"Careful is my middle name."

"Not any more," Freddie said.

———

Tree parked at the side of the Traven house and then dashed through the rain up the steps. Elizabeth answered, barefoot, hair tangled, wearing a toga-like shift that didn't fall past her thighs. The drink in her hand dispelled Tree's initial thought of Phaedra, besotted with her stepson. More like Elizabeth, a little drunk and scared.

"Dwayne Crowley's been released from jail," she announced. He expected thunder to rumble.

"How did you hear?" Tree shut the door and followed her across the foyer.

"My husband called." She raked her free hand through her hair. "He's coming here. I just know it."

Tree said, "The police know he's out. They'll keep an eye out for him."

"Keep an eye out for him?" She sounded appalled. "You think the police are going to lift a finger to help me?"

She stared at him accusingly, as though he was responsible for the lack of police assistance. "Go into the other room," she said. "I'll come right back."

Outside the big living room windows, nature mounted a sound and light show that could open in Vegas. He watched until he saw Elizabeth's shifting reflection in the window.

She held a fresh drink in one hand, a gun in the other.

"What are you're doing with that?" He wasn't talking about the drink.

She thrust the gun into his hands, a .38 caliber revolver. He stared down at it. "What am I supposed to do with this?"

"You stupid bastard. You're supposed to protect me with it."

"I don't know anything about guns."

She put her drink down and came toward him, breasts moving beneath thin fabric. Her arms slipped around his neck.

"What are you doing?" was all he could think of to say before she kissed him. She tasted like whiskey.

In the detective novels he read as a kid, the hard-boiled private eye—Shell Scott, Mike Shayne, Mike Hammer—always resisted the femme fatales's advances. Tree could never understand that. How could they resist these hot, compliant women? Why would they resist?

All these years later, a detective of sorts himself, and here he was resisting Elizabeth Traven, Captiva Island's resident femme fatale, pushing her away, announcing in a lame voice, "I'm a married man."

Elizabeth hit him. His nose exploded in blood. His glasses went flying. She pummeled him, blood spraying the carpet. He fell to the floor. She was on top of him, screaming unintelligibly, flailing haphazardly but nonetheless landing a few blows. He managed to grab her arms and swing her off, pinning her to the floor.

"You're bleeding on me, you asshole."

Straddling her, he let go of her arms so he could wipe his bleeding nose.

"Get off me you fool, get off." She was weeping now, her face slick with her tears and his blood.

He fell away from her. She rose to her knees, body shaking with the force of her sobs.

Elizabeth stumbled to her feet, pulling at the hem of her shift, reaching for Kleenex in an elegant ivory case on a glass-topped coffee table. She threw a wad of tissues at him. They floated like pink kites. He grabbed a couple and held them to his nose. He saw his glasses on the floor, surrounded by bright red blood spots.

"You've got blood all over the carpet," she said. "What kind of detective are you, anyway?"

"The kind that bleeds."

He retrieved his glasses and then hoisted himself to his feet holding the tissues against his nose.

"What's wrong with you? You can't even be seduced."

"What are you doing trying to seduce me?"

She flared angrily. "Why does anyone do it? Because they want to get laid. Don't you know anything?"

"I don't think you want to get laid, Elizabeth. Not by me, anyway."

She dissolved into more tears.

"Hey, it's okay," he said. "I'm not very seducible these days."

"You're such an idiot," she said between sobs. "Why do you think I hired you in the first place?"

"To have sex?"

She issued a derisive snort. "You've got to be kidding."

She flopped onto a nearby easy chair, alternately pulling at the hem of her shift and brushing away tears. He offered her a tissue.

She blew her nose. He dabbed at his. The bleeding had pretty much stopped.

"We knew the boy had been to see you," she said. "Do you understand? This was a way of getting you on side, that's all it was."

More sobs exploded out of her. He handed her another wad of tissue. "I've had too much to drink," she said angrily. "I shouldn't be talking like this."

Her chin bobbed up and down. "I told my fool husband not to give you that money, that it wouldn't change anything. Sure enough, it didn't. So here we are tonight."

"Where are we, Elizabeth? What are you talking about?"

She was sitting up, holding her head in her hands. "I don't

want you hurt, you or your wife. You're just a couple of harmless idiots who stumbled into this."

"I know that the woman I found, Dara Rait, she dealt in body parts. Mickey Crowley and Reno O'Hara are part of it. So was Mickey's husband, Dwayne."

"Yes," Elizabeth said.

"Brand must have met Dwayne in prison. You hooked up with Mickey. Mickey brought in Dara Rait."

Elizabeth lifted her head away from her hands. "We needed a liver, just part of a liver, actually."

The penny dropped. "For Brand's niece."

"Hillary. To save her life. Marcello turned out to be the perfect match."

"But Reno went crazy for some reason and killed Dara, and suddenly everything was a mess."

"He thought she was cheating on him."

"With Mel Scott?"

"I have no idea."

"Marcello was scared of what they were going to do to him, so he ran away. He didn't want an operation. He figured if he could find his real mom, everything would be all right. That's when he came to me."

"These people are worse than camp guards in the Gulag," Elizabeth said. "After you found Dara's body, I tried to get them to go away, but they wouldn't listen. They are greedy and petty and ruthless. They won't stop until it's finished."

"Until what's finished?"

"The operation, for God's sake! That's what all this is about." She staggered to her feet. "I should never have had so much to drink. God, what have I got myself into?"

He grabbed Elizabeth's arm, twisting her around to face him. "What operation? They don't have Marcello. How can there be an operation?"

"You fool. Don't you get it yet? This is why you're here. Dwayne's at your place. He's taking the boy."

"Where? Where are they taking him?" His voice was high, angry. A voice he had not heard for a long time.

"It's too late," she mumbled. "You can't stop them."

"Where?"

She threw up her hands, an exhausted heroine in a dreadful stage melodrama playing to the last row in the house. "Some place near Fort Myers Beach. A mobile park. That's all I know."

Tree found the gun on the floor where he dropped it when she attacked him. He picked it up. "Is it loaded?"

"Of course it's loaded," she snarled. "What the hell good would it be if it wasn't loaded?"

He stuck the gun in the belt under his shirt. It fit nicely, he thought as he went out into the rain, hurrying down the front steps. He hated to think in clichés such as his heart beat like a drum. But that's what it was doing. He was a gun-toting detective on his way to save the love of his life, heart pounding.

At the bottom of the stairs Detective Mel Scott materialized out of the darkness. Tree came to a stop. "Am I glad to see you," he said.

Scott stepped forward, placing his weight on one foot so that he could slam his fist into Tree's stomach.

The breath went out of him. He sank to his knees in the rain, the gun falling out of his belt, clattering to the wet pavement.

"Look at that," said Scott sarcastically. "Our hero detective is packing."

Cee Jay Boone bent down and picked up the gun.

35

Mel Scott yanked Tree to his feet and together with Cee Jay Boone hustled him over to a nearby SUV and pushed him into the rear. Scott got in beside him, jamming a gun into his ribs while Cee Jay slipped behind the wheel and started the engine.

"Looks like Mel's not working undercover after all," Tree said.

Mel said, "Shut up."

They shot out the front gate onto Captiva Road, the rain intensifying, the sound of beating windshield wipers punctuating the silence.

"Where are we going?" Tree managed to gasp between the spasms of pain shooting through his stomach.

"Shut up," repeated Mel Scott. He rammed the gun harder into Tree's ribs. Cee Jay glanced at the rearview mirror.

"I tried to warn you to stay out of this. You can't say I didn't warn you."

"You warned me as in 'stay out of this Tree, for your own safety.' Not, 'I'm a corrupt cop, Tree, and I will kill you if you get in my way.' I might have listened to that."

"Too bad for you asshole," Mel growled.

"What I don't understand is how a couple of supposedly street-smart cops like yourselves got mixed up with Reno and his gang of losers."

Mel chuckled. "Pal, you really are new to the scene. Any time you're involved with bad guys, by definition you are mixed up with losers. But sometimes the losers have the money. That's what you're after. You got to be a little smarter, that's all."

"I could be wrong," Tree said. "But driving me through the rain with a gun in my ribs while Dwayne and Mickey kidnap Marcello and my wife, that doesn't strike me as very smart."

"Mel, shut him up," said Cee Jay tightly, eyes glued to the road.

"Last time, shithead, keep quiet."

"What are you going to do, Mel? Kill me?"

"Yeah, that's exactly what I'm gonna do."

Tree kept quiet.

———

In the darkness, Tree wasn't sure where Cee Jay turned, but suddenly they swerved off onto a gravel roadway framed by low hedges. A lightning flash illuminated a grassy shoreline dipping into a shallow inlet. The car crunched to a stop. Cee Jay twisted around to Tree.

"Get out," she said.

"What are you doing?"

"Telling you to get out of the car," she said in a tense voice.

Mel Scott shoved him into the door, then reached across to pull at the handle. The door flew open, spilling Tree onto the roadway.

Tree was on his knees, realizing he'd lost his glasses. He groped in the darkness, panicky, desperate to find them. No luck. Cee Jay got out of the vehicle. Mel joined her, shining a flashlight at Tree. He raised a hand to deflect the glare.

Mel said, "See that boat over there, Tree? I want you to get on your feet and walk toward it."

"I don't see any boat," Tree said.

"Tree, just do it," Cee Jay said.

Tree got to his feet, his mind whirling, trying not to worry about lost glasses, concentrating on ways to save himself. He needed to be inventive. But he couldn't think of a damned thing. He stood rooted to the spot in the rain until Mel delivered a stinging backhand.

"Get moving."

His ears ringing, Tree, lurched forward.

"I can't see the boat," he called out to the darkness.

"Sure you can," Mel Scott called back.

"Where is it?"

"Keep moving Tree," Mel said. "Just a little further."

There was no boat. He knew that. They were going to kill him. They were going to do it, right here in the pouring rain. He vaguely wondered if he would even hear the gunshot before the bullet roared into his head.

Something moved in front of him against the downpour.

Mel was right behind him, giving him another shove. "Come on," he said.

A voice said, "Tree, get out of the way."

Tree ducked to one side.

Mel moved his gun hand up. A shot went off. Tree, crouching away, couldn't tell who fired. Mel dropped his gun and pitched forward.

"Get down!" Savannah Trask was shouting at frozen Cee Jay. "Down on your knees, now!"

Cee Jay, not as foolish as her partner, complied, slowly sinking to the ground. Savannah moved past Tree. "Down. All the way!"

Cee Jay sprawled flat on her stomach.

"Hands behind you," Savannah commanded. She glanced at Tree. He noticed the gun in her hand. "You okay?"

Was he? The ex-girlfriend who broke his heart now saved his life. An ignominious turn of events, but he wasn't about to complain.

"Pick up Mel's gun," she said, the same way you might ask someone to pick up a quart of milk. Tree dutifully retrieved the gun.

The rain let up, reducing itself to a hazy drizzle as Savannah moved in on the prone Cee Jay, producing a pair of handcuffs like magic. She tossed them to Tree who should have caught them, as they do in the movies. But he missed the catch. He shoved Mel's gun into his pocket and quickly bent to retrieve the cuffs. Not far away, Mel Scott shifted and groaned.

"Attach one of the cuffs to her wrist," Savannah ordered. When he complied, she said, "Now attach the other to her friend Mel. They can be together until I get help back here."

Tree hoisted Cee Jay up and dragged her over to where Mel lay unmoving. He grabbed his arm up so that he could snap the other handcuff to his wrist. Cee Jay glared but said nothing.

Tree turned to Savannah. "They've got my wife and the boy."

"Then let's go and get them." As in, let's go for a walk or let's stop at the supermarket. As if she rescued wives and children all the time.

"Agent Trask!" Cee Jay's voice sounded muffled. "You can't leave us here like this!"

"Don't you just love the dialogue?" Savannah said.

They went along the trail to where Mel had parked his SUV. Savannah's Jeep was a few feet behind it.

"How did you know where I was?"

"I followed you," she said.

"Why would you do that?"

"Because I knew what you were going to do."

"How could you know what I was going to do?" The notion angered him. "You don't know me, Savannah, you never did."

She stopped and turned to him. "I know you better than you think. Even when I was young and silly and wondered what it would be like to seduce every boy in the world, I knew there was only going to be trouble if we stayed together."

"Except you got into more trouble after I left."

That made her smile. "I guess it depends on what you think of as trouble."

"How about getting involved with Reno O'Hara and having a baby with him? How's that for trouble?"

To her credit, she managed to hide any hint of surprise. "That certainly would be trouble, if it were true."

"Come on, Savannah. That's why you're here. You're trying to find your son. You're trying to find Marcello."

"You're not making a whole lot of sense, Tree." Her voice had lost its confident edge.

"I kept the love letter."

"Love letter? What love letter?"

"The letter you wrote me."

She was silent a moment. "I never wrote you a love letter, Tree. For the simple reason I was never in love with you."

"You also wrote Marcello. He showed me the cards you sent him. The handwriting is the same."

She opened the driver's side door of the Jeep, paused, and turned to him. There were tears in her eyes.

"What is it?"

She reached to touch his face. "Things lost," she said.

The Jeep windshield exploded, spraying him with glass and blood.

36

A second explosion blew out a headlight. Tree caught a glimpse of Savannah, half her head gone, thrown back against the Jeep. He leapt into the darkness. Warm swampy water enveloped him. Vaguely, he heard another explosion.

Then he was beneath the water, kicking furiously, trying to get as deep as he could. He hit the spongy bottom, reaching blindly to grab the weedy grass undulating against him, pulling at it to propel himself along.

Finally, when he could stay under no longer, he broke the surface, shooting up into a tangle of mangrove roots. He hung amid the cable-like roots, not moving, breathing quietly. Wet earthy smells. Night sounds. Drizzling rain on water. An echoing breeze.

Slowly, carefully, he moved forward through the muck, pushing at the roots, squeezing through them, crawling up an embankment to find himself back on the road. He rose to his haunches, looking around, listening. Nothing. He started along the road, crouching, keeping close to the mangrove.

He came to a toll booth beside two portable washrooms. He stopped to catch his breath. He heard something. Footsteps on gravel, coming toward him along the trail.

Directly to his right lay a narrow wood bridge. He ran to it and crossed, his feet thumping against the boards. The bridge ended but the walkway continued, twisting through the encroaching mangrove. He reached a second bridge. On the other side, he came to a stop, holding his breath. Listening. He could hear someone coming.

Tree started running. The walkway twisted again so that he could see a structure that became the rear of the Ding Darling Education Center.

He ducked past cement pillars and found himself beneath the building's overhang. Iron railings were piled against a wall. To the right was a fire door with a reinforced window panel. If he could somehow get inside, there would be a telephone.

He picked up one of the railings. Holding it like a club, Tree smashed at the glass. It cracked and buckled but held. Tree swung harder the second time, splintering the glass. He reached inside, hit the roll bar, and the door sprung open.

As he came up the stairs, an alarm bell started ringing. Good. That would bring the police. He just had to survive until they arrived. No big deal. Simply because his pursuer killed an FBI agent a few minutes before, and was anxious to kill him, didn't mean he had anything to worry about.

He went through another fire door and found himself on the main floor. Faint light illuminated hanging birds, and a pelican mounted in foliage. One of the exhibits promoted "The Changing Estuary." "Seeing the Unseen," promised another display. Well, he would know in a minute or so, wouldn't he? Behind him, he heard a clatter. A hulking figure darted through the fire door—Dwayne Crowley, the jailhouse naturalist, paying a visit to the Ding Darling Wildlife Preserve. Like so many visiting tourists, Dwayne had brought along a sawed-off pump-action shotgun.

Tree dived behind one of the exhibits a split second before the roar of the shotgun spread buckshot through the room, shredding a display board devoted to the history of the mangrove cycle.

Tree glanced up and saw he was adjacent to the replica of Ding Darling's office. Ding's cartoons and drawings were scattered across his desk near his eyeglasses, evidence Ding would soon return to render more beautifully drawn, wonderfully ascerbic cartoons, India ink masterpieces that captured so well the foibles of man.

The original swivel rifle used by poachers in the 1930s hung in its usual place on the wall above Ding's desk. But the replica carefully reconstructed by Rex Baxter and friends, sat on a floor mount behind a roped-off portion of the office. It was shinier beneath the indirect lighting of the twenty-first century but otherwise looked exactly like the long-barrel gun used so many decades before by the illegal market hunters.

Tree heard echoing footsteps. Dwayne was coming.

Dwayne with his shotgun.

Tree grabbed at the long-barreled rifle.

The footsteps grew closer.

With great effort, Tree lifted up the rifle, swinging it awkwardly around, his finger clawing at the trigger.

Dwayne drifted into view, indistinct, but clearly the same pumped and tattooed dude Tree had encountered in Naples. Dwayne held the shotgun loosely in his hands, a man unconcerned by the evening's challenges, a professional getting the job done.

The only problem was that ringing alarm. Sooner or later it would bring the cavalry. By that time, Dwayne Crowley would be far away.

Then Dwayne spotted Tree, his eyes going to the gun the length of a railway tie, a gun you see once in a lifetime, if that.

That brought Dwayne to a halt.

Tree noted the look of blank surprise on the ex-convict's hatchet-like face. A sixty-year-old guy, soaking wet, covered in sand and grit, pointing this ancient blunderbuss at him, the last thing he expected.

Tree had no idea what would happen when he pulled the trigger. He was as surprised as Dwayne when the big gun detonated with a kick so powerful it propelled Tree backward. Three pounds of buckshot hit Dwayne, punctuating him with dozens of small holes, lifting him off the floor into a display case.

Tree figured Dwayne must have been dead before he hit the floor.

37

The rain had pretty much stopped by the time Tree parked on San Carlos Drive. He lifted Dwayne Crowley's shotgun off the passenger seat and got out of the Jeep. Dara Rait's mobile home sat in the misty darkness of the Bel Air Motor Park.

He'd run back to the Jeep—ignored Cee Jay Boone's hysterical entreaties to be freed from the semi-conscious Mel Scott—found the key still in the ignition, and all the time tried not to look at Savannah's limp body, tried not to think of what he was doing or remember who she was and what she had meant to him. He did his best not to dwell on the fact that a few minutes before he had done the unthinkable and killed a man.

Him. Tree Callister. Killing someone. Who was this guy, anyway?

No time for any of that. Just get to Freddie. Crawl behind the wheel and start the Jeep's engine. Don't think of anything else.

Except Freddie. Nothing else mattered but Freddie.

———

A distant Roy Orbison sang "Only the Lonely." Tree inspected Dwayne's shotgun. One cartridge remained in the chamber. To do what? He wondered. To do what was necessary, he told himself.

The interior of the mobile home remained dark. If anyone was in there, they were certainly being quiet. He slipped over to a dumpster adjacent to the trailer and crouched behind it. After a couple of minutes huddling there, feeling slightly foolish, he crept across to the front steps. The entrance door was locked. He cursed himself. Absolute fool that he was, he had gone to the wrong place in order to rescue the damsel in distress and save the day.

Then he heard something—noise coming from the trunk of the car parked at the side of the motor home. He stepped closer, not sure he was hearing right.

Again: *Thump! Thump! Thump!*

He opened the driver's door, found the trunk release, pulled until he heard a metallic pop. He went back and gingerly lifted up the lid. Freddie lay on her side, duct tape over her mouth, hands tied behind her back. The edges of her hands were bloody and scraped where she had been hitting against the underside of the trunk.

Tree lifted her out. Her wrists had been bound with plastic strips. He twisted them off. Her hands free, she tore at the duct tape, finally ripped it off her mouth, breathing hard, weeping softly.

"Good grief," she said. "Good goddamn grief, Tree. You came for me."

"You thought I wouldn't?"

"How was I supposed to know?" Brushing away tears. "It wasn't exactly listed in the marriage contract."

"Oh, yes it was. You didn't read the small print. Third page, fourth paragraph down: 'Husband will rescue wife as needed.'"

"I missed that part." She kissed his lips and that made everything he had been through so far tonight worthwhile.

"Where are they? There's no one inside the trailer."

"They went off down the street with Marcello," she said.

"Let's go and get him."

"I've got a better idea. Let's call the police."

"You always want to call the police," he said. He started for the street.

She called after him, "Tree," and then ran to catch up. "You haven't got your glasses."

"No," he said.

"Can you see anything?"

"I only need them for reading."

"What's that?" She indicated the shotgun.

"It's a shotgun," he said.

"Where did you get a shotgun at this time of night?"

He wondered when there was a better time to get shotguns. "It belongs to Dwayne Crowley. He tried to kill me with it."

"What did you do?"

"I'm not entirely sure, but I think I killed him."

They passed barriers marking off the road construction in progress. Beyond the construction a sign said "Maryland Cottages." Eight of them, abandoned on either side of a roadway going toward the Matanzas Pass Bridge. A white van was parked just off the road.

"That's the van they brought us here in," Freddie whispered.

The forlorn little cabins were all but lost in the shadow of the bridge, the white paint peeling, brown porches sagging. Seven of the eight cottages were dark and empty. The eighth cabin at the end was lit.

As they approached, the front door opened. Mickey Crowley stood framed in the light spilling onto the roadway. Mickey stared at them. Tree opened his mouth to say something but before any words could get out, Mickey whipped up her Beretta Tomcat and did what she probably wished she had done the first time they met—she shot him.

It felt as though he had been hit by a two-by-four. He staggered back, dropping the shotgun, trying to stay on his feet, everything swirling. Through the blur, he saw Mickey clatter down the steps, gun held out, getting ready to shoot him again.

Then Freddie stepped past him with the shotgun.

Ka-boom!

The blast ripped through the porch railing, missing Mickey completely, but startling her enough that Tree was able to recover and slam into her, knocking her back against the cottage. She tried to scramble away. Freddie used the shotgun like a club to hit her. She screamed, which provoked Freddie to hit her again.

Tree snatched Mickey's Beretta off the porch and lunged into the cabin.

Under portable halogen lights, two men in green hospital scrubs were poised on either side of a narrow operating bed. Marcello lay beneath a sheet. A ventilation mask covered his face. An IV line snaked away from his right arm. One of the hospital-gowned men held a scalpel. They stared indignantly at Tree.

He pointed the gun and said, "Put your hands up." A sentence he never in his life expected to utter. Both men immediately complied. The power of the gun.

Trying to keep the room in focus, Tree issued a further command: "Move away from the table."

The two men did as they were told. The one on the left said, "We are about to operate on this boy." He spoke with an accent. Of course, thought Tree. The evil doctors would have accents.

"You're not operating on anyone." The words sounded garbled to his ears. Neither of the men said anything. Then Freddie brushed past him and lunged at the table.

"Get that mask off him," she snapped. "And remove the IV line."

"You shouldn't do this," said one of the doctors.

"We're taking him to a proper hospital," Freddie said. One of the doctors removed the ventilation mask. The other unhooked the IV line. As soon as this was done, Freddie lifted Marcello off the table.

She said, "Come on, Tree, let's get out of here."

With Marcello nestled in her arms, she swept out the door.

Tree shook his gun at the two men as he started to back up. "No one moves!" he shouted.

Another sentence he never expected to utter.

He stumbled outside. Freddie in a hazy ring carried Marcello to the van. She opened the rear door and carefully laid him inside. Then she came back to Tree and put her arm around him. His shoulder hurt. He leaned against her. "I don't feel so well," he said.

"Probably because you've been shot."

She got him into the passenger seat and then went around and climbed behind the wheel. Everything was moving so slowly, he thought. He felt nauseous.

"Freddie, I think I'm dying," he said.

"You're not dying, my love." Her voice seemed far away.

"What makes you so sure?"

"Because we still have a long life ahead of us."

"Do you love me?"

"Forever," she said.

The car jolted forward. His last thought before he lost consciousness was, Forever? Isn't that nice? In that case, maybe he could live.

38

He got his job back. After everything that had happened, this was the best news yet. He would be a reporter again, and everything would be as it was, in the place where he was most comfortable. All he had to do was report to the newsroom in the morning.

Tree arrived at the side entrance and hurried up the stairs. He found himself in sales and circulation. This was strange. What was he doing here? He thought this was the newsroom. He stared around. No one paid him the slightest attention. He tried to ask for directions. The newsroom. Where was it? He had to get to the newsroom. People stared blankly. They didn't seem to know what he was talking about.

He got out of there into a stairwell, climbed another set of stairs and went through a fire door. Now he was in a room full of linotype machines. Linotype machines? No one used linotype machines anymore. What the hell was going on? The clack-clack of the machines filled the air. It was stifling in here. He could hardly breathe. An old man wearing a green visor hobbled over, waving copy paper in his face. He yelled over the incessant metallic clack of the machines. "You stupid young bugger! You don't know how to spell Mississippi!"

Tree reeled away. No. This was impossible. He couldn't have misspelled Mississippi, not on his first day back at work.

He staggered along an endless row of linotype machines working at full noisy tilt. Where was the newsroom? How could he start work if he couldn't find the newsroom? And how could he misspell Mississippi? He didn't even have a story. How could he work at a newspaper if he couldn't find the newsroom, and he couldn't spell Mississippi, and he didn't have a story? Deadline must be approaching. He had to have a story. What time was it? He didn't have much time left.

And he couldn't find the newsroom.

Tree jerked awake and saw that he was still in his hospital room. With a combination of relief and sadness, he realized there was no job. He was not the newspaper reporter reborn, merely the Sanibel Sunset Detective shot. And hurting. His arm was in a sling and he was attached to heart monitors and a breathing apparatus.

A voice said, "You were sleeping."

Tree looked over at the hazy figure of FBI Special Agent Shawn Lazenby seated by the bed, neat and professional in a dark suit and matching tie, his hair in a shiny pompadour.

"Weird dreams," Tree said.

"I'll bet." Lazenby folded his hands in his lap, tidy and compressed. "What with all you've been through." Was that a note of sympathy Tree detected? Hard to tell looking at Lazenby. His face remained as neatly arranged and free of emotion as the rest of him. Nothing showed with Lazenby, Tree thought. Until it did show.

"Or age," Tree said. "I think the dreams have more to do with getting old."

"I wanted to see you before I left," Lazenby said.

"At least you're not here to kick the shit out of me," Tree said. "Or are you?"

"I owe you an apology for that. Jealousy. Also, I was on painkillers. Pretty silly on my part."

"You were in pain?"

"What?"

"The painkillers."

"A different kind of pain, you might say."

"Savannah tended to have that effect on people," he said. "She could even convince an agent who was in love with her to spend time on Sanibel Island helping her find her lost son."

"Yes, I suppose she could." Lazenby's voice remained steadily in neutral, refusing to sound surprised about anything Tree might know.

"How much trouble are you in?"

"I'll find out more when I get back to Miami this afternoon, but I'm probably finished with the agency."

"I'm sorry to hear that."

"I did love her, although I don't think she loved me. But that's all right."

"I wonder if Savannah loved anyone," Tree said.

"She loved her son, and maybe you, too."

"Shawn, Savannah didn't love me."

"I wouldn't be so sure," Lazenby said.

"As for Marcello, you know more about that than I do. The fact she let him go off with a character like Reno O'Hara gives you pause. What was she doing mixed up with him in the first place?"

"She felt she had no choice at the time but to let O'Hara take the boy. She lost track of them for several years before she found out they were in the Fort Myers area. As for O'Hara, I guess he was more evidence of how much Savannah liked to walk on the wild side. One of the reasons she joined the FBI, I suppose. But in O'Hara's case, she paid a pretty high price."

That reduced them both to silence. Lazenby got to his feet.

"I'd better get out of here. I've got a long drive ahead of me."

"Good luck," was all Tree could think of to say.

Lazenby allowed a hollow smile. "For what it's worth, you surprised her."

"Being a detective? I don't doubt it."

"Not that so much. The fact that you found something like happiness here. That unsettled her a bit, I think. She didn't know what to make of it."

"I am happy," Tree said. "Whatever happiness is. I'm shot but I'm happy."

"I'm real glad for you, Mr. Callister."

"You take care of yourself, Agent Lazenby."

"Yes, sir. You too."

Lazenby left. Tree lay back in the bed, thinking about his dream. Not being able to find the newsroom, that was crazy. Of course he could find the newsroom again. That is, he could if he ever went back. But he would not be going back. Every time he turned to gaze into the past he saw smoke plumes rising from the distant burning bridges of his life.

He lay there a while longer, becoming tired again, thinking he once beheaded the wrong king of France in a story he wrote. But he didn't think he'd ever misspelled Mississippi.

Had he?

39

"George Clooney is a movie star," Rex Baxter said a week or so later. He sat across from Tree in his office. The two of them sipped the Grande Lattes Rex brought in from Starbucks.

Tree shook his head. "George Clooney looks like a movie star. He acts like a movie star. If he had come of age in the 1950s or 1960s, he would be a movie star, maybe the rival to Newman or McQueen. But the sad fact is, George Clooney is not a movie star."

"Why do you say that?"

"Because he can't do the one thing movie stars must do."

"Which is?" said Rex.

"He doesn't make hit movies. This is not the age of the movie star. This is the age of computer-generated images. Therefore, someone like Clooney is lost. He doesn't make studio movies these days. He makes mostly independent films that in this sad time most people don't see. Regrettable, but that's the way it is."

"So there are no movie stars? Is that what you're saying?"

"Meryl Streep is a movie star. So is Sandra Bullock. These women attract a female audience still interested in stars. They are not interested in CGI and explosions."

"So the only movie stars are women?"

"The only stars in the time-honored sense, yes. But that's all right. Women were the first movie stars, anyway. Florence Lawrence and Mary Pickford. Shirley Temple in her day was a bigger box office draw than Clark Gable."

Rex frowned and heaved himself to his feet. "I can't sit around here trying to make you listen to reason. I gotta get over to the mall and listen to some guy who owns an outlet store bitch about his membership dues. You okay?"

"I'm fine."

"There's been a whole lot of negative publicity, you know," Rex said unhappily. "Murder on Sanibel Island. Shootings. Not good for business, Tree."

Rex sounded as though he held Tree personally responsible.

"If I was Paul Newman, it would be fine."

"Yeah, but you're not Paul Newman."

"Funny. When Paul Newman died, that's when I knew."

"Knew what?"

"That there was no hope for any of us. Paul Newman stayed young forever. He defeated time and age for so long. And then he died. Where does that leave the rest of us?"

Before Rex could answer, Tommy Dobbs, wearing a black suit and looking like one of the Blues Brothers in his Ray-Ban sunglasses, appeared at the office door. "All set, Mr. Callister?"

Rex looked at Tree and shook his head. "What? You've got a chauffeur now?"

Tree motioned to his arm in the sling. "I can't drive like this."

"Make sure you don't shoot anyone," Rex said. "I've got enough trouble."

"I can't shoot anyone until the arm heals."

"Thank goodness for small mercies," Rex said.

Tommy and Tree went down the back stairs and out into the parking lot where they encountered Ray Dayton. He said to Tree, "Do you suppose we could have a word in private?"

Tree turned to Tommy. "Why don't I meet you at the car?"

"Okay, sure." Tommy gave Ray a mystified glance as he walked away.

Ray said, "How's the arm, Tree?"

"Still a little sore, Ray."

"So you've taken a round," Ray said. "Well, that's a step in the right direction, isn't it?"

"Yes, I've always wanted to be shot."

"But it was basically a scratch, right?"

"Well, it broke my arm." Did Tree sound defensive? Maybe the Ray Man would appreciate Tree more if the shot had killed him. He would have liked that just fine.

"Let me ask you something, Ray. Where were you in Vietnam?"

"What?"

"Vietnam. When you were there. Where were you?"

"I wasn't in Nam."

"You weren't?"

"Philippines. I ran a supply chain."

"You fed people?"

"They couldn't have fought the war without guys like me."

Tree tried to think of something to say. He couldn't think of anything.

"Todd, myself, a couple of the boys from Kiwanis, we're doing a little fishing this weekend out in the gulf. Few beers, few laughs. We might even drop a line in the water. Thought you might like to join us."

Tree wasn't sure he'd heard correctly. "You want me to go fishing with you?"

"You're not busy, are you?"

"Not particularly, no."

"Then come along with us."

"I'm not going fishing with you, Ray."

The Ray Man's face hardened. His eyes got smaller. "Hey," he said. "I'm trying to reach out to you here."

"I appreciate that, Ray. But I'm not going fishing with you."

"Look, you hit me. Fine. Maybe I deserved it, I don't know. You had your moment. Now you're a local damned hero, shooting bad guys, screwing up tourism. Good for you. But I need Freddie back at work."

"You'll have to talk to Freddie."

"This is crazy what's going on. Things happen. It's water under the bridge. Tell her that, okay?"

"Water under the bridge?"

"I want her back at work." He turned and marched off across the lot. He had a funny kind of quick step. Like a duck in a hurry.

Then Ray stopped. He turned to Tree and called out to him. "None of this changes my opinion of you."

Tree said, "How do you spell Mississippi, Ray?"

"What?"

"Never mind."

Ray recommenced his curious duck march.

40

Nothing had changed at the Brand house except the "For Sale" sign in front. An elegant "For Sale" sign, Tree noted. Things could only be for sale elegantly in this neighborhood.

He climbed the steps to where Jorge waited. The major domo had the good manners not to comment on the sling holding Tree's arm as he led the way through the foyer and into the living room. Elizabeth Traven was artfully arranged in a shaft of morning sunlight. The hellion with the wild hair and long legs was nowhere in evidence. The plantation matriarch was on duty.

They stood, eyes on each other, in awkward silence. Finally, she said, "Well, you don't look too much the worse for wear."

"Winged me, as they used to say in the cowboy movies."

"I don't watch cowboy movies," she said.

"I'm shocked," Tree said.

"I understand you knew the FBI agent who was killed."

"Savannah Trask. We lived together for a time when she was a law student."

"And she is the boy's real mother?"

"So it seems. She had been involved with Reno O'Hara in Chicago. They had the baby together. She gave up custody when she was transferred to Miami."

"Curious. A woman giving up her child like that."

"She'd taken a leave of absence to come here and find her son. So had her partner, Agent Lazenby."

"So obviously she'd had some sort of change of heart."

"Obviously."

"How do you feel about all this, Mr. Callister?"

"I don't feel very good, Mrs. Traven. It was all so unnecessary."

She scrutinized him as though trying to ascertain how to handle this; what tact to take in an encounter she had not expected.

"Let's sit outside," she said. "It's such a pleasant morning and who knows how much longer I'll be able to enjoy it."

"I see you've got the house up for sale."

"There's no money. Well, that's not totally true. But there's certainly not enough money to hang onto this place."

A vast lawn floated off toward a tidal bay and the clear, straight horizon of the sea. They sat on lovely white rattan furniture beneath a bright green umbrella. Hillary Traven drifted by, a tiny stork in the distance. She saw the two of them and waved.

"How is she doing?" Tree said.

"What's the term they use? As well as can be expected? That's it."

Jorge appeared as though conjured from a puff of smoke, to ask if they wanted anything. Elizabeth suggested coffee and Tree went along. Jorge withdrew. Pink spoonbills skimmed the grass near the water.

"When I'm not dealing with Trotsky, I've been reading all about you."

"The reporter got carried away."

"Quite the hero."

"Are you disappointed?"

"In a way, I suppose I am," she said. "I did not expect you to rise to the occasion."

"No one is more surprised than me."

"I suppose the world needs more people like you, Mr. Callister, people whose grasp occasionally exceeds their reach—and they get a nice write-up in the local paper."

"So how are you holding up, Mrs. Traven?"

She turned her face toward the sea. "Trouble and more trouble; my husband's fight to get out of prison; this last bit of nonsense; unhappy bankers; avaricious real estate agents. Lawyers added to lawyers; platoons of them. I can't keep their names straight. I have no idea how we're going to pay for them. But they don't seem to worry so why should I?"

She gave him sidelong glance. "The little bit of good news, at least from my perspective, they've decided not to prosecute me."

Jorge returned with a silver coffee service. They were silent while he went through the ritual of asking Tree what he wanted in his coffee, and then pouring milk, adding sugar for Elizabeth, leaving them both staring at china cups they did not touch.

"The only thing that keeps me from getting really, really pissed at you, Mrs. Traven, is knowing why you did all this." He nodded in Hillary's direction. "That whatever you did, you did for her."

"Yes," she said, delivering another of her trademark rueful smiles. "Sometimes, like you, I surprise myself."

"It's just that you have a funny way of going about helping."

"We didn't think we had a lot of choice. Hillary has a rare liver disease. Biliary atresia. When she was a child they treated it with an operation called the Kasai procedure. It worked, but then eighty-five per cent of children with the disease need a liver transplant within the next twenty years. So sure enough, by the time Hillary turned twelve, she was in a terrible state and in urgent need of a transplant."

"But the right liver was not available," Tree said.

"What's more there was a very long waiting list. Hillary couldn't wait. We had to do something."

"By now your husband was in prison. I thought that's where he would have met Dwayne Crowley. But they were in separate facilities."

"That's right."

"It was you, Mrs. Traven."

She looked at him without comment.

"Maybe you were feeling lonely and miserable, I don't know, but you found your soul mate in Dwayne Crowley at Prisonlife.com."

Her face darkened. She kept her eyes firmly on Hillary, down on her haunches, intently watching the birds as they fed along the shore. When Elizabeth spoke again, her voice was barely above a whisper.

"Stupid, stupid, stupid. I can't believe just how stupid I acted. I can't imagine what I was thinking. But you're right. I was lonely and frustrated and angry. I was rummaging around various prison websites, trying to come to terms with where my husband was and what it meant. I stumbled across Prisonlife.com quite by accident. Dwayne struck just the right chord in the state I was in—a strong, reassuring voice in the night. Just what I needed—or thought I needed."

"Dwayne put you on to his wife, Michelle."

Elizabeth nodded. "Mickey introduced me to Reno O'Hara and Dara Rait, body parts dealers in South Florida. Illegal but reliable. The way of the world these days. If you want something, you have to be willing to pay for it."

"They had the perfect donor, a boy your niece's age."

"They would even provide the Mexican doctors willing to perform the operation for a price. One-stop shopping. We were desperate. Hillary was going to die if we didn't do something."

"Marcello, however, didn't want to go along. He didn't want to have a scary operation and so he ran away. He was determined to find the mother who had been writing, promising to come for him."

"Unexpectedly resourceful. Somewhat like yourself, Mr. Callister."

"No, Marcello is much better than me, better than I could ever imagine being," Tree said. "To do what he did, to survive the way he survived. He's an amazing kid."

She lowered her eyes and said, "Yes." The only intimation of guilt or remorse she allowed herself.

"Anyway," Tree continued. "Reno murdered Dara and that threw a wrench into everyone's best laid plans. Something had to be done. Reno had to be removed."

"Dwayne?"

Tree shook his head. "It looks as though Detective Mel Scott did the honors, revenge, I suppose, for what Reno did to Dara, the woman he'd fallen in love with."

"All of a sudden there are bodies turning up everywhere," Elizabeth said. "I couldn't believe what was happening. I'm in the middle of some sort of inter-gang feud."

"That's when you should have pulled out," Tree said.

"I didn't feel I could. I felt I had to make the best of a dreadful situation."

"So you helped them out by coming to me. You became a client hoping to get to Marcello."

"As I said Mr. Callister, I didn't have a lot of choice."

He stared at the white china cups on the white table. The coffee remained untouched. The spoonbills had deserted the tidal basin. A breeze played with the tendrils of Elizabeth's hair. A beautiful, troubled woman, he thought, whose difficulties were far from over.

It was as though she read his mind. "I don't need your sympathy," she snapped.

"I know you don't," he said, standing. "But you've got it, anyway. And Marcello's too."

"What's that supposed to mean?"

"He wants to donate part of his liver to Hillary. That's what you need, isn't it?"

"Yes," she said, not able to keep the surprise out of her voice. "I guess the question is why?"

"Now that he knows about your niece, that a liver transplant will save her life, he wants to help."

Momentarily, she was at a loss for words. "Marcello would do that? He would give Hillary part of his liver."

"Yes."

"That's astonishing," she said. "What made him change his mind?"

"He didn't know what was happening. Everyone was angry and threatening. He thought his mother was coming. All sorts of things were swirling around. If someone had taken the time to speak to the boy calmly and reasonably, explain the circumstances, simply love him, all this might have been avoided. Instead, bad people scared him, and so he ran away."

She stood up, emotions playing on her perfect features that included vulnerability—but mostly relief.

"We will pay him, of course."

"You probably don't have the money," Tree said.

"We will find it. Maybe we won't pay a couple of rich lawyers but somehow we'll find it."

"Marcello doesn't want your money. He has no real concept of it, anyway. He just wants to help."

"I don't know what to say," she said.

"The next time you see Marcello, just say 'thank you.'"

They stood looking at one another, exhausted fighters who had punched each other to a standstill.

Hillary Traven, shimmering among the spoonbills, waved at him as he left.

Tommy Dobbs waited behind the wheel of his car as Tree came down the steps. He reached over and opened the passenger door and Tree slid inside.

"Thanks for waiting," Tree said.

"No problem, Mr. Callister. No problem at all. Where to now?"

"Drop me over at Lighthouse Beach."

41

When they got to the beach, Tree said, "Let me off in the parking lot, Tommy."

"No problem, Mr. Callister. Anything I can do for you. That's fine."

He pulled the car to the stop. Tree looked at him. The car idled. Tommy stared ahead, swallowing hard, Adam's Apple bobbing.

"What's wrong?"

Tommy glanced at Tree. "Nothing's wrong."

"Tommy."

"Why does anything have to be wrong?"

"You're being too nice. You're not asking questions. You're not tweeting. You're not on Facebook. You haven't videoed me. What's going on?"

"I've been downsized, okay?" His Adam's Apple moved faster.

"Downsized?"

"Yeah, downsized. Let go. Whatever you want to call it. I'm out of a job."

"Why? What happened?"

"They're 'restructuring,' they said. They've got to make cuts. Necessary to keep the business viable. I'm the last man in so I'm first out."

"But you've done such a good job for them."

"They don't care. What do they care?"

Tommy lowered his head. Tree didn't know what to do except wrap his arm around him. He sank against Tree's shoulder, knocking off his Ray-Bans. Tree was conscious of sitting in a parking lot adjacent to Lighthouse Beach holding an unemployed newspaper reporter. He reached down and picked the sunglasses off the floor. "You've got two eyes."

Tommy looked at him. "What?"

"You said you wear sunglasses because you've only got one eye. You've got two."

"Oh."

Tree handed him the Ray-Bans. Tommy said, "I've got a funny eye."

"What's funny about it?"

"It wanders. I look straight at you, I'm not actually looking straight at you."

Tommy demonstrated. Tree said, "You look all right to me."

"It's not right."

"I think you're going to do fine, Tommy."

Tommy cleared his throat and replaced the Ray-Bans. "You better get out of here, Mr. Callister. You'll be late."

"What are your plans?"

"Stay with my folks in Tampa till I get back on my feet. That'll be okay, I guess. My father and I, we don't get along so that makes things kind of tense. But it'll be all right. It'll be fine."

"Listen, keep in touch. I'm not sure I can do anything, but I'll make a couple of phone calls, see what's around."

"That would be great, Mr. Callister. I sure will stay in touch, don't you worry about that."

Tree groaned inwardly.

———

A beach sky, blue and cloudless, brought out the tourists. Tree marveled at the numbers of people baking beneath the unrelenting sun. That lucky old sun could kill you, could it not? But then so could pump-action shotguns and women with Beretta Tomcats.

Marcello, on his knees, maneuvered a big yellow sand shovel near the lapping surf. Freddie, spectacular in her orange one-piece, sat not far away, reading the one love letter Tree ever received. The duck's beak of a baseball cap shaded her face. The sunglasses made her look like Jackie Onassis. He knelt and kissed her mouth. Marcello beamed happily at him and then went back to his sand shovel.

"How did it go?" Freddie folded the letter, and removed her glasses.

"It went fine," he said.

She handed him the letter. "Written by a woman in love."

"I don't think so," Tree said.

"I do. Women know about these things. She was in love with you."

"No, Freddie, you're in love with me. That comes out in a hundred different small but telling ways every single day. We're in love with each other. We don't write letters and then go off with other people. It's straight and true and simple. This—" He waved the letter. "This is so many words on paper. They don't mean anything unless you back them up, and Savannah didn't do that. You know what? She didn't even remember writing it."

"Marcello says he would like to go to Savannah's funeral or whatever kind of service they're holding for her."

"I've talked to the police," Tree said. "They've been in touch with Savannah's parents in Chicago. They're going to let me know what they decide. I suspect FBI Agent Sean Lazenby will want to be there, too."

"How's he doing?"

"Pretty broken up, and in trouble with his bosses for taking unauthorized leave so he could come here with Savannah. Crazy, but he was in love with her, like everyone else."

"You included?"

"Whatever it was with her was a long time ago. Lost to the mists of time."

"Lost to the mists of time? Good grief."

"The best I can do on short notice."

Marcello came over. Tree said, "Mrs. Traven can't believe you want to help her niece. She's thrilled and very thankful."

"What's her name?"

"The niece? Hillary. Her name is Hillary. She's about the same age as you."

"As long as they don't hurt me," he said.

"They won't hurt you. No one's ever going to hurt you again." The sentence came out with a lot more emotion than he intended.

Freddie laid her hand on his arm gently. "We said we'd meet them at two thirty."

"Can't we stay here a little longer?" A pleading note in Marcello's voice.

"We'll do this again very soon," Freddie said. "But right now we want you to meet the people who are going to take care of you."

"All right," Marcello said.

"Incidentally," Tree said to Freddie. "The Ray Man wants me to go fishing with him."

"You're kidding."

"He was in the parking lot at the office."

"He's crazy."

"He also wants you back at work."

"You're not going fishing with him, are you?"

"He wasn't in Vietnam."

"He wasn't?"

"He ran a supply chain in the Philippines."

"He fed people?"

"They couldn't have fought the war without him."

They collected towels and sunscreen and flip-flops and Marcello's sun hat and his sand shovel, packed everything up and started off the beach.

"Are you going back to work?" Tree asked.

"Are you going fishing?"

They looked at each other and laughed. Marcello reached up and took Tree's hand. Tree found himself swallowing hard. Freddie slipped beside him and leaned against him as they walked, squeezing his arm.

"The detective from Sanibel Sunset Detective," she murmured.

"What about him?"

"He's a cry-baby."

"What a thing to say to a hardbitten hombre like myself. I've been shot, you know."

"Why do I suspect I'm never going to hear the end of this," she said.

———

They drove across the causeway off the island, along Summerlin Road to McGregor Boulevard until they turned onto Cypress Lake Drive and found the address they were looking for—a pleasant one-story stucco house with a red tile roof. It was occupied by an equally pleasant-looking couple, Mr. and Mrs. Calvin Lake, a forty-something black man and his wife with a shy daughter, Carmine, age eleven. She hugged against her mother until ordered to take Marcello inside and show him his bedroom.

Immediately, she darted forward and grabbed Marcello's hand, grinning broadly. "Come on," she said, pulling him toward the house.

They got as far as the stoop. Marcello stopped and broke free of Carmine's hand and ran back to embrace Tree with all his might. The tears rolled freely down Tree's cheeks as he hugged Marcello. Freddie brushed away her own tears.

Then Marcello was gone, following Carmine into the house. Tree clumsily cleared his throat. Freddie extracted more promises from the Lakes. They had spent their lives raising foster children, they said. They weren't perfect but they were pretty darned good. They knew what Marcello had been through.

Tree and Freddie walked hand in hand back to their car. They got inside, Freddie behind the wheel, and they sat there until the Lakes disappeared inside and their world altered perceptibly because it no longer contained Marcello. He was, finally, safe.

Neither of them spoke on the drive home, enjoying the silence and the closeness of each other. They were back on the causeway, its sweep captured in the afternoon sunlight glinting on the choppy tips of the waves in San Carlos Pass.

"It's funny," Tree finally said. "I see the island and I feel like we're going home."

"We are going home," she said. "This is home."

She glanced over at him. "You okay?"

"Of course I'm okay. I'm a hero or haven't you read the newspapers?"

"Oh, Lord," she said.

"I don't know whether I mentioned it. Did I tell you I've been shot?"

A rogue tear tumbled down his cheek.

"What is it, my love?"

"Just now. I was overwhelmed by this terrible feeling of sadness," he said.

"Because you have to put up with me for the next fifty years?"

"No, because we have passed things that we will never come back to again," he said. "Because we are closer to the end than we are to the beginning."

"But we go on anyway," Freddie said. "On and on together."

He reached for her hand and she reached for his, and they drove along like that, holding hands, the Florida sun shining over their island, going home.

ACKNOWLEDGEMENTS

In the late 70s, working as a magazine writer, I went down to Murrell's Inlet, South Carolina, to interview the mystery writer Mickey Spillane. Spillane had created private detective Mike Hammer in the 1950s, setting off something of a firestorm with such hardboiled classics as *I, the Jury*, *My Gun Is Quick*, and *Vengeance is Mine*.

The novels were full of sex and violence, or so my parents thought. I could not be exposed to such things—so, of course, I secretly devoured the paperbacks, reading under the covers by flashlight late at night, enthralled.

I had met Spillane a few years before in Toronto and we got along, so he insisted I stay in his rambling oceanfront house. He was single at the time and had plenty of room. Mickey introduced me to two things that have stuck with me ever since. He was the first person I knew who had CNN, the new twenty-four hour cable news network, and he kept it on all the time. I thought that was pretty nifty—TV news any time you wanted it.

He also introduced me to catfish at a local restaurant. When he initially suggested it, I was horrified. "Just try it," he ordered. "I swear you'll love it." He was right, and I've eaten catfish ever since. Every time I do, I think of Mickey.

After dinner that night, he showed me to the guest bedroom which, as I recall, doubled as the office where he continued to pound out manuscripts—rather incongruously he had just written an adventure novel for young people.

On the desk beside the bed stood the battered typewriter he used to write the original Hammer novels—a single draft written in days, never reread. The walls were filled with blowups of the lurid pocketbook covers that beguiled me almost as much as the books. Hung over the back of the chair beside the bed was a shoulder holster containing a .45 automatic, the same gun Mike Hammer used in the books to pump lead into the broads and hoods who offended his sense of justice. The original Signet paperbacks lined the shelves adjacent to the bed.

I grabbed *I, The Jury*, the first Hammer novel, tucked myself into bed, pulled the covers over my head and began to read, the same way I had as a kid. Here I was in Mickey Spillane's house, a .45 nearby, cocooned under the covers, once again lost in the rough, tough world of the private detective—childhood fantasy bumping into adult reality to create a certain kind of late night bliss.

I thought about that time with Mickey Spillane a lot as I wrote *The Sanibel Sunset Detective*. He would not have thought much of Tree Callister, although when you got to know him, Mickey was such a disconcertingly kind and gentle man I doubt he would have said anything. Still, the vibrant memory of my long-ago infatuation with the pulp novels, not only of Spillane, but also of such practitioners of the craft as Richard S. Prather, who wrote the Shell Scott novels, and Brett Halliday, who wrote the Mike Shayne mysteries, were sources of inspiration.

I did not even try to reproduce the sort of hardbitten hero those authors created (inspired, of course, by the much more literary work of Dashiell Hammett and Raymond Chandler). However, I did want to emulate their no-nonsense storytelling. They got to work each day churning out words, keeping the story moving, working overtime to ensure the reader had no distractions beyond turning the next page.

If I was fortunate enough to come even close to what these masters seemed to achieve with such effortlessness, I have editors Ray Bennett and Alexandra Lenhoff to thank. They saved me from myself any number of times. My wife, Kathy Lenhoff, read the manuscript in its earliest incarnations and again just before it went to press. She inspires me in so many, many ways far beyond these meager literary efforts. Also, my son, Joel Ruddy, John D. MacDonald fan extraordinare, blessed the manuscript, thereby encouraging me to keep going.

In Florida, I received help from everyone I encountered on Sanibel and Captiva Islands, two of the most gloriously beautiful and unusual Florida paradises. Particularly helpful, as always, was my brother, Ric, who not only provided insights into life on the islands, but also corrected the manuscript if my characters veered left when they should have turned right. Any lingering mistakes, however, are mine alone.

Friend and neighbor Kim Hunter introduced me to Naples, Florida, and unknowingly provided one of the novel's locations.

I would also like to thank the very talented Bridgit Stone-Budd who went to extraordinary lengths to create the book's cover. And of course West-End Books publisher Brian Vallée. Overwhelmed with his own work, he nonetheless selflessly took time to come to the aid of a friend.

Mickey Spillane died in 2006 at the age of eighty-eight. Today, he is all but forgotten, part of a fading era, as are Prather and Halliday, not to mention Erle Stanley Gardiner, and even John D. MacDonald, those great paperback writers who helped me navigate adolescence. They live on in sweet memory, though, by flashlight, under covers, late at night.

Coming Soon

A new Tree Callister adventure

THE SANIBEL SUNSET DETECTIVE RETURNS

Find out more at
www.ronbase.com

Contact Ron at
ronbase@ronbase.com

CPSIA information can be obtained at www.ICGtesting.com

225937LV00001B/3/P